# A Gathering
of Days

# A Gathering of Days

## A New England Girl's Journal, 1830–32

*A novel by Joan W. Blos*

Aladdin Paperbacks

Aladdin Paperbacks
An imprint of Simon & Schuster
Children's Publishing Division
1230 Avenue of the Americas
New York, NY 10020

First Aladdin Paperbacks edition 1982
Second Aladdin Paperbacks edition 1990
Also available in a hardcover edition from
Atheneum Books for Young Readers

Printed in the United States of America


Library of Congress Cataloging-in-Publication Data

Blos, Joan W.
    A gathering of days : a New England girl's journal, 1830–32 : a
novel / by Joan W. Blos.—1st Aladdin Books ed.
        p.    cm.
    Summary: The journal of a fourteen-year-old girl, kept the last
year she lived on the family farm, records daily events in her small
New Hampshire town, her father's remarriage, and the death of her
best friend.

    [1. Diaries—Fiction.   2. New Hampshire—Fiction.]   I. Title.
PZ7.B6237Gat   1990
[Fic]—dc20   90-32   CIP   AC


ISBN 0-689-82991-4

*Sarah's book*

## Acknowledgments

Much of the reading for this book was accomplished at the New York Public Library, the Graduate and William C. Clements Libraries at the University of Michigan, and the town library of Holderness, New Hampshire. Also consulted were town and county records in Holderness and Wolfeboro. I am grateful to these facilities, and for help received.

I have discussed parts or aspects of the story with past and present members of the Department of History at the University of Michigan. I appreciate their interest and their insights.


*Joan Blos*
*Holderness, New Hampshire*

# A Gathering
of Days

To my namesake, Catherine:

I give you this book on your fourteenth birthday, as I turned fourteen the year of the journal; the year that was also my last on the farm tho' I did not know it then. It was also the year that my father remarried, and my best friend, Cassie, died. Cassie lives in my memory still, of all of us the only one never to grow old.

Once I might have wished for that: never to grow old. But now I know that to stay young always is also not to change. And that is what life's all about—changes going on every minute, and you never know when something begins where it's going to take you.

So one thing I want to say about life is don't be scared and don't hang back, and most of all, don't waste it.

Your loving great-grandmother,
Catherine Hall Onesti

## I

Sunday, October 17, 1830

I, Catherine Cabot Hall, aged 13 years, 6 months, 29 days, of Meredith in the State of New-Hampshire, do begin this book.

It was given to me yesterday, my father returning from Boston, Massachusetts, where he had gone to obtain provisions for the months ahead.

My father's name is Charles: Charles Hall. I am daughter also of Hannah Cabot Hall, dead of a fever these four long years; and older sister to Mary Martha whose dark, curling hair resembles our mother's, but I have our mother's blue eyes.

My dearest friend is Cassie. The Shipmans' farm lies *South* of ours, and is rather larger. Cassie is older than I by a year, but the same in height. We tell each other every thing; and each of us in the other's dear heart finds secret dreams reflected. Cassie's brothers are: David Horatio, older by a full two years; Asa Hale, my age exactly; and William Mason, the youngest. He is but a baby and called by every one "Willie."

This day being the Sabbath we attended services both morning and afternoon.

Tuesday, October 19, 1830

This be the precept the teacher set out today:

> . . . let thy words be plain and true to the
> thoughts of thy heart.

These be the thoughts of my heart: that I may remain here for ever and ever; here in this house which my father has built with the labour of his two hands;

that no harm come to those I love: Father and my sister, Matty; Cassie, and the Shipman family; and Father's brother, our Uncle Jack, who mills when he needs money, and never took a wife;

also that I may train myself to want to do what I am asked to do;

last, and most bitter of all to confess, I wish that my hair were curly, as Matty's is, and our mother's.

Thursday, October 21, 1830

Teacher Holt commended me for writing with a finer hand than I have displayed before. Still must my capitals be improved, achieving a better flourish.

This night Father told us a story after the supper hour. A man had lost four hogs in the woods and went there to retrieve them. Before he had gone very far on his way a headless woman rose up before him—spectral, and blocking the path. As might be expected he fled the spot. But thinking on it when he woke to the morrow, and still much the poorer for the loss of the hogs, he ventured back again. There he discovered that his apparition was naught but the rooty tangle of a fallen tree! Animals had gnawed some portions away, thus suggesting the shapes and the shading, and the woman's arms, as he had supposed, were but a pair of larger roots, bent at an equal angle.

The lesson, as Father put it to us, is that intelligence must prevail for had the fellow not returned he'd have suffered all his days, victim to an ignorant fear—no better than the meanest man, or least instructed child.


Friday, October 22, 1830

We had a visitor today but nearly failed to admit him. No callers, surely, were expected. And peddlars, tinkers, and the like will not come by till Spring. Thus we ignored the rattling latch—at times the wind will mislead us so —until a voice called out.

It proved to be our Uncle Jack and tho' he protested he was just passing by, I thought he meant to visit. He brought some store sweets, wrapped in paper, and consented to have some cyder.


Tuesday, October 26, 1830

Winter is coming on! There was ice across the trough this morning, and frost on the upper meadow.

Uncle Jack to visit again. Father could scarce believe 'twas so, but Uncle Jack had read in the paper where a Mr. Sam'l Newell had raised a white potato to better than 24 inches, taken in girth around! But here comes our uncle with the paper itself, and printed just as he told it. Then nothing would do but down to the cellar to hunt and search for the largest of ours, and carry it up for measure, amidst much speculation.

When I could wait the supper no longer, having earlier raised the pot from the fire but still was scorching threatened, I ventured to invite our guest and soon set out a pleasant meal, Uncle Jack joining gladly.

Later Father praised me direct, saying that I was a pride and a comfort, and added directly after *that*, "There's many a full grown woman here would not do as well." I shall not forget his words and am resolved that for all my days I shall assay such tasks and virtues as may sustain his comfort and increase his pride.

Monday, November 1, 1830

Only three more weeks remain until Thanksgiving Day! I must attach my new lace collar to my Sabbath dress. Also, it being snug for me, I must take up the patterned frock which I have given to Matty. She can use it nicely, I think, together with her new knit stockings and the red Morocco boots that were mine once also.

Cassie and I and Mrs. Shipman have already begun the preparations for the Thanksgiving meal. The cakes we make first are those that keep best in the cellar's cool. Last week we turned out some gingerbread; today we made a Yankee Cake and a firm Plum Pudding. Mrs. Shipman's sister in Salem had sent a new receipt for this, but as we had no currants here we had to do without.


Thursday, November 4, 1830


Returning home from school this day I had a dreadful fright! Clearly I saw presented to me the dark silhouette of a lanky man, his coat all tattered against the sky, his bony hand above his eye as if to give it shade.

Although I quickly pointed him out, so swiftly did he vanish away that nothing remained when Cassie and Asa obeyed my pointing finger. Then, stumble-tongue'd, I must explain what I had wished them to see.

Asa remembered the story I told her of a headless woman and that story's teaching. From this he determined that nothing would do unless we followed after. Cassie, ever more prudent, demurred; therefore must I, as the third of the party, cast the deciding ballot. As it was coming on to dark, and I still had our supper to set, I announced with Cassie. Asa, at this, scowled ruefully. But soon thereafter we all joined hands, & in most perfect companionship resumed the homeward journey.

Friday, November 5, 1830

Along the road and in the fields is neither green nor white of snow; all is sere and brown. How much farther one can see, now that the leaves are gone! Only the faithful evergreens guard the margins of our fields and keep the forest secrets.

"Look, Cath," Matty calls to me, her small face muffle'd and cold. "My breath is frosting like Babe and Nelly's!" Then she lows, as oxen will, till I am quite ashamed.

Saturday, November 6, 1830

Mrs. Shipman called on Father. The purpose was to present to him that her sister will visit from Salem. Now she called her "the unmarried one" and said she would stay a while. Of this he assured her he was glad, and hoped they both would enjoy renewal of old and sisterly ties.

There being nothing further to say, they spoke of other matters. He will build the cupboard she needs. She, exchanging service for service, agrees to provide continued instruction in the diverse household arts to myself and Matty. " 'Tis hard," she sighed, "the loss of a mother, and her gentle guidance."

"We do all right," I heard him say. "Now I've no wish to offend you, Em. But we do all right," he repeated.

November 7, 1830. The Sabbath Day.

Uncle Jack, and we three also, visited with the Shipmans after morning service. Mr. Shipman and Father remarked how frequent are the instances of bound boys run away. When they were lads, or so they say, it was much less common. Now each week's *Courier* displays a greater, and more petulant, number of master's advertisements. "Will no longer be responsible for," "any having knowledge of," "the subscriber wishes to state . . ."

"And what would you do," our Uncle Jack asks, "were such a fellow hereabouts, and known, by chance, to you?"

"Turn him out and turn him in," is Father's prompt reply.

"But Charlie," Uncle Jack pursues, "supposing the boy were right to run off—"

"He couldn't be that, to my way of thinking; bound being bound to stay. Besides, I'd not want to intermeddle—no, you'd *have to do it*, and do it clean; send the vagrant, whatever his claim, back where he belonged."

Father believes, as he's often said, that man's intelligence is given to him that he may distinguish right from wrong, and knowing right, may do so. Some think him too severe in this. It is not that, but honour.

# ❧ II ❧

Wednesday, November 10, 1830

I saw my phantom again today—this time it stayed a longer while, peering and peering into the dusk, and in the same location, over by Piper's Woods.

I am resolved to examine the spot, and prove myself to A. and Cassie, both inclined to teaze me still, about my apparition. "Now, Cath," they'll say, "what headless being will you find today?" Or: "Have you stray'd hogs, Catherine Hall, to take you in to the woods?"

Sophy told us today in school her father says when she turns fifteen she's to be sent to Lowell, Massachusetts, there to work in the mills. The Perkinses are badly off, and as she's strong she could make good money; being also healthy and well used to hard work.

But Sophy to go to Lowell? I should be quite terrified to be thus torn from all I love—people, place, and ways.

Sophy says the recruiter said the houses there have parlours for the girls, and are very well kept. Some of them even have pianos! Sophy is musical—like all of the Perkinses—and oft will sing so prettily when her father fiddles. I dare say she will learn to play and soon delight them all.

Friday, November 12, 1830

> Why are a scolding woman's hands
> and a fur cap alike?
>
> (Both will warm your ears.)

Tuesday, November 16, 1830

Joshua Nelson was thrashed in school. What he had
done was not half so bad, or so Teacher Holt explained, as
that he sought to put the blame on another scholar. After
the thrashing he had to write, "To thine own self be true"
on foolscap one hundred times. (It is from a play by Mr.
William Shakespeare who, Teacher Holt explained, lived
and wrote in England, 1564–1616.) "To thine own self be
true." Teacher Holt believes that very much; and so do I, I
think.

Saturday, November 20, 1830

Mrs. Shipman's sister arrived last night—very late but
in good spirit despite her lengthy journey. It was nearly
mid-night when the coach reached the bridge where, her
arrival being expected, Mr. Shipman met her and fetched

her belongings home. She left Boston at three in the morning, having travelled there from Salem.

How odd a sight, in the Shipmans' yard, so stylish a figure from bonnet to boots, waving & chatting from the wagon seat, and all by flaring torches of pitch to ward off the mid-night dark. She strongly resembles Mrs. Shipman, although much younger in years.

I and Cassie were allowed to await her actual arrival. Thus I saw the large trunks she brought, each of them capacious. Also of hat boxes more than a few; I know as I carried them in!

Today she showed us the gifts she brought: lengths of sattinett and cassimere, and several of *Godey's Lady's Books* that Cassie's mother may sew a best dress in the style of her choosing. Trims of lace and braid there were too, and a set of real jet buttons . . .

Cassie and I simply fell on the *Books* and, tucking under our school girl collars, quickly pretended to cloaks and gowns of the latest fashion!

Monday, November 22, 1830

The weather appearing very severe, we were early dismissed from school. Afterwards Cassie called on me, bringing along the stockings she's knitting, and wrapped so well in her mother's shawl I almost mistook her figure! We sat pleasantly, side by side and scarcely noted the gathering dark, so busy were tongues and fingers.

Cassie showed me, as she'd recently learned, to knit *a*

*long hair* with the yarn when one turns the heel. This will give it added strength, and so prolong the wear.

Sophy has told me she admires A.; but Cassie, when I told her of it, observed that Sophy need hardly *confess* what anyone could see. As for Asa he cares for her not, and mocks her little simper and nose-that-wrinkles ways.

Cassie and I are quite agreed: we'll not reveal affection until certain of its return.

(Apples are excellent this year. We enjoyed several to-day.)

Tuesday, November 23, 1830

As the snow continued we did not go to school. Later, when it had abated, I cleared the pathway to the barn as a help to Father. It is quite uncommon to have snow so deep so early.

Thanksgiving Day, 1830!

Such a feast as we had at the Shipmans, with food till we could eat no more, and divers pies aplenty! Also the pudding, and the Yankee Cake, and the gingerbread!

Uncle Jack set us all to laughing, pretending he simply could not decide *which* of these sweet cakes he liked the best, & tasting of each repeatedly "to know where to place my approval." Still at the table Willie fell asleep, then was carried off to bed, with his stockings on.

Aunt Lucy—we are to call her that, same as the Shipman children—Aunt Lucy wore her dark green silk, the one she wore the day she came, and laughed and chatted with every one, of a merry crowd the gayest. Cassie's mother wore her old dress but brightened it with lace at the cuff from Aunt Lucy's supply. Also were the jet buttons used, which sparkled from Cassie's Sabbath-day best and made it look quite new. My collar received good admiration, and Matty *would* hike up her gown and skirts the better to show the boots.

Father seemed not lost in thought, as is often his manner. He added many a witty remark and, with Matty upon his lap as the evening drew to a close, oft held the party's eye.

Then is it wrong to wish we might, one day at our house and table, exchange the parts of hosts and guests as we have so long played them?

## III

Sabbath

Weather was inclement. However we went twice to church where, as he will ever do, Priest Fowle's dog barked noisily at the late arrivals. 'Twas odd to *see* the dog at this office for the cold was so severe it rendered each breath into puffs—bark! puff! bark!

Monday, November 29, 1830

I have searched just every where! Today I carried my writing book home—Father had said he wished to see it, and Teacher Holt had granted permission exactly on that account. Now neither I nor M. can find it, looking with care throughout the house and in unlikely places.

I do recall that I set it down next to my cap and muffler and mittens as we started home. We only paused but once on the way, and that to pick some pods and grasses close by the side of the road.

I have not yet told Father of this: and how will I tell Teacher Holt how I've misused his trust. I pray the book be safe where it is and that I find it tomorrow!

Tuesday, November 30, 1830

Aunt Lucy hurried 'round today—we were so newly returned from school she must have noted the very moment when Cassie and Asa reached the house and then set out for ours! It was not me she wished to see, nor Matty for that matter. But here she came, all bundled up, and asking Father as he'd harness to mend—or so she'd heard from Mr. Shipman—would he, and so forth, be so kind as to repair the leather strap which she now put forward? It had *somehow* rent apart, and came from one of her trunks. Father queried as he took it if she'd soon be leaving?

"O my no!" she answered him, her voice gone high and not her own and both hands vaguely waving.

"Well, it's no trouble either way. I'll have it right in a moment."

But she'd already removed her cloak and fanned her fingers to the fire, lightly moving the kettle aside with a practiced gesture. Aunt Lucy knows her way at a hearth and, as I've observed at the Shipmans', cooks most tastefully. But in our house there was naught to do, *nor* would Father engage her in talk but sternly attended to his needle and its linen thread. Matty stared quite openly; but I made a show of inspecting closely some trousers of Father's that he'd put by as being in want of mending.

Now did Aunt Lucy, speaking too brightly, wish aloud she'd brought handwork along with which she might *join* the party. None of us more than nodded at that, and Father soon presented to her the firmly over-stitched strap. Aunt Lucy thanked him prettily and then she had—or so she said—truly to be leaving. Father spoke lightly as he fastened the door behind our departing guest.

"Do you suppose we ought to've asked if she wished a bit of cyder?"

Matty, too, had a question to ask; hers not of her own devising. "Are you going to marry Aunt Lucy? Sophy says her mother says that's what you ought to do."

"You tell Sophy," Father said, and poked a thread through his needle, "you tell Sophy *and* her mother we're doing fine just as we are. Would you not say so, Cath'rine?"

I nodded contentedly in agreement, liking the way he said my name, and pleased by his approval. "So if the ladies are wanting a wedding—" I rose and swung the kettle back, as he continued speaking—"they'll have to find them another man, if not another maid." He looked as if he might go on; did not, and fell to stitching. Presently he began to sing, putting in hums where he missed the words which for Father happens often.

Wednesday, December 1, 1830

I can not think what has *transpired*; still is my lesson book missing. Fortunately none seemed to notice that I wrote my lessons on foolscap pages. I was in fear of discovery all the day.

Did another scholar mistake it? Surely he would have brought it to school—unless kept home on some account, & will bring it tomorrow?

The pond ice being thick and black, as will happen when cold persists with no snow between, we disported there after school. When we girls grew weary of skating, the boys cut branches of evergreens, and quickly pronounced them royal sleighs upon which we might ride. How festively we laughed and called, pretending we were ermine'd queens, and leaning back against the boughs while, before us, the boys' long strokes carried us over the ice.

Among us only Sophy was spilt. Worse than that, when she tumbled over, you could see her pantaloons! I should have died of shame, I know, had it befallen me. And worse, still, than the pantaloons, it was revealed to one and all that Sophy ties, around her stocking, a piece of scarlet ribbon.

Thursday, December 2, 1830

Lo! my lesson book is returned, and in the queerest way!

There is a nubbly boundary stone that separates the school house lot from the woods that belong to Wally Piper where both lots front the road. My book was there at the close of school, just as plain as any thing, as if it had been set down. At first I dared not trust my eyes, certain it could not have fallen there, and who, I asked, would place it thus, and in such risk of harm?

However, I dwelt not on such thoughts, but taking it gladly in to my hands turned the familiar pages, each of them a friend. Then, on the cover's inner side, just below my name and the place, a stranger and intruder amidst that company:

PLEEZ MISS
TAKE PITTY
I AM COLD

The letters seem drawn with charcoal and are raggedly formed. I know not what to make of it, nor can wait to tell Cassie and Asa.

Friday, December 3, 1830

I could not speak with them. Sophy met up with us on the way & dogged our steps to school. Returning, Matty had a cough; must go directly home. I supposed she had taken a chill, the weather being harsh of late, and she but a bit of a child.

Arriving, I blew the fire up, then out to the pump to fill the kettle, and hung it to the flames. While we waited for it to heat I rubbed her feet between my hands and kept her warm with blankets. The water ready, I wrung out a flannel, sprinkled it lightly with turpentine, and laid it on her chest. This I did to prevent the cold from taking firmer hold.

Mrs. Shipman, hearing of illness, came 'round to offer help. However, she found all I'd done in order and did not amend the treatment.

M. is resting now.

Father ought to be soon returned, as it is close to dark. Today he is logging with Mr. Shipman, down toward the pond, I think.

Saturday, December 4, 1830

When I stepped out to the yard this morning a bit of paper held beneath a stone promptly attracted my eye. Altho' my fingers were clumsy with cold I hastened to smooth it open.

"Wait at the rock," it said. Altho' it lacked a signature, I knew the writer was Asa.

*What* rock, however, and *when* ought I wait? No other meaning seeming to fit, at last I concluded that A. knew *some thing* about my lesson book. Could *he* be the one to have taken it? No, it seemed not likely. Mayhap, its reappearance? I knew I could not puzzle it out; therefore with what *eagerness* did I await our meeting! How hard it was to not begrudge Father and Matty the time they took with their preparations and the morning meal. 'Twas a little of this and a little of that and "Catherine do stop fidgeting, it makes a man uneasy!" I thought he never had tarried so long over common meat and cakes—and asked for bacon too! At last with all in tidiness I set out for school.

The sky had brightened, giving light, when I came to the rock. The wind, tho' light, seemed to glaze my cheek, and brought tears to my eyes. I stood there clapping my feet together—they taking turns to be clapper and clapped—and marking how thin are the soles of my boots, never intended for frozen ground or standing about of a morning. Had he been there before me or would he not come? Had I misread Asa's message? At last I heard the school bell ring and knew I could wait no longer. Public mortification now compounded my woes. On account of my late arrival I must pass before all the scholars, and so to my place. My face turned red as a smithy's in summer! Teacher Holt did not rebuke me. He must have seen the extent of my shame, considered it sufficient.

During the recess interchange, when girls going out meet boys coming in, Asa contrived to approach me. "After school! In the same place." Then he must pass on.

There is so much more to tell. But I can write no longer now; shall resume tomorrow.

The next day

I followed A. in to the woods, he having appeared as he said he would, and soon showed me the boot prints he'd found near where I'd seen my phantom. They were sharp, and deeply imprinted, as if they'd been made when the ground was soft, then caught fast by a freeze. Clearly a man's boots they were as to size; the prints themselves being widely spaced to suggest a long-legged stride.

"Whose?" I asked.

"O, Cath! You know! Your phantom and no other!"

"But this would be a *real* man, Asa; no mere vision'd phantom. What manner of man do you suppose—"

"A black man you said, at least dark complected. I'd supposed a run-away slave come to here for hiding."

"A Negro, Asa? We've had none before, neither slave nor free. So I couldn't know what it might mean to call him dark complected." Tho' I tried to give lively argument I knew him to be right. "*Any* man will leave prints where he walks, and these say naught of his colour. Perhaps it was just a run-away lad not liking his indenture."

What Asa liked not was my timid suggestion. "No," he asserted, "it need not be a poor Negro slave! It might be a thief, or a man convicted. Maybe he was meant to hang, and escaped to our woods? Is that what you would have him be, rather than a slave? Besides, what difference would it make—"

Behind Asa's figure I saw tall trees, and hidden by them what manner of man; where in these woods might he be? Then Asa looked at me levelly and I, staring back, to return his gaze, noticed as I never had that one of his eyes is lighter in colour than is its companion!

"It doesn't really matter," he said. "Suppose that he was wrongly convicted and this his hope of freedom, a good life later on."

I was in such a whirl! Asa was saying, "Whoever he is, he's cold and needs us to help him, Cath. Who are we to judge?"

Thus was it revealed to me that Asa had found my book on the rock and read the inscription there.

But Asa's father had not said, "Turn him out and turn him over."

"Asa," I said, "we must go home. I have to think on it."

(I have not spoken to Cassie yet; intend to do so tomorrow.)

# ❧IV❧

Sabbath-day, December 12, 1830

I could not speak with C. today, her mother keeping close by her side at morning service, and after.

I am so mindful of the stranger—every thing reminds me of him—the cold we felt on going out, the grateful warmth of home. Yet sadly I am in no way nearer to knowing what is right, in this instance, and what I ought to do.

"Please, miss . . . I am cold." Sinned against or dangerous sinner? I do so long to speak of it, yet who can give me counsel? "I am cold . . . Take pity." I wish he had never come to our place, disturbing the quiet of our woods, enforcing his words in my book!

Monday, December 13, 1830

Some of the Shipmans' pies are stolen, that had been put in the buttery after Thanksgiving meal. They were meant to freeze and keep, and would have been good till March.

Asa, whose sweet tooth is well known, was thrashed for the offense. Cassie, who does not know of the phantom, observes that A. protested but little, and that this is a confirmation he was indeed the culprit. As I am quite certain 'tis the phantom's work, again are wrong and right confused, and by what plausible signs.

Asa's brother David noted that the footprints in the snow matched not Asa's boots. But there was Asa, accepting guilt—this to protect the phantom I'm sure—and Asa's father brushing him off, saying that yesterday's snowfall was fine and, what with the wind and drifting over, no print would hold its shape. "Besides," he said, "like charity, stealing begins at home."

## Tuesday, December 14, 1830

In this day, under skies so blue they seemed entirely to mock me, I have despaired, have been enlightened; and, at what ought have been the height of my joy, been again cast down. I have so sorely offended Cassie she will not speak to me. I can not remember that this has happened before.

Before a chance was provided to me Asa spoke with Cassie about what we had seen in the woods. I knew when I crossed the school house sill, how terribly she disapproved; the eyes that found me were dark and troubled, and scarce consented to mine.

My mind, as I took my seat, was distress'd—and not with the lessons ahead. To disregard both Father and Cassie? I thought I could not do it. But how could I refuse the pleas of Asa and the stranger? The first of these so fully persuaded, the other so much in need?

Teacher Holt took his usual place, setting out precepts for the youngest to read in words of one syllable.

"Give to them that want," he wrote. The text seeming chosen to address my dilemma, how my heart leapt up! I poked at Cassie in the row ahead and she, tho' slightly, nodded.

Several other precepts appeared below the wondrous first. Then:

"Speak the truth and lie not."

Cassie turned to me at this, sorrowful & rebuking. Forgetting myself I exclaimed aloud, "But no lie is asked!"

Thus was our teacher's attention drawn and, I composing my face the faster, Cassie was chastised.

"Think you, Miss Shipman," said Teacher Holt, making the title a taunt, "think you, Miss Shipman, that you, or I, or indeed *any* of us outgrow these simple school room teachings? No, 'tis their very simplicity that makes them last, and last, and last. And therefore will I have you write—one hundred times that you may remember: teach me to do Thy will."

Cassie, the purest in spirit of all to be so cruelly shamed! Slowly, how slowly, the day wore on. I could not risk a sign or gesture and this was truer punishment than any a teacher might have devised to fit the circumstances.

For Cassie, it now seemed to me, had been in the right. The very *concealment* were a lie; and Cassie, because obedient and good, had known at once what I, and Asa, were so slow to see.

Going home I walked abreast of her, carefully matching my step to hers, hoping she might send me a glance that I might return with a smile. But she, so gentle, was adamant; and turned at her gate without speaking.

Cassie! Cassie! Will you hear your friend? Cassie, will you forgive me?

O! in the morning will all be told, and will you then accept me back who am so undeserving?

Thursday, December 16, 1830

Cassie said, "Forgive me, Catherine."

"No, 'tis I," I begged.

At length, amidst what stinging tears, we each of us heard the other out—for even as I had taken her view, so surely had she, in sleepless hours, come to accord with mine. Such turnabout evoked wan smiles; and when, at last, we spoke again Cassie said so quietly it was nearly a whisper, "Kindness must be the highest virtue—don't let me forget that ever. Were I to strive for one thing only 'twould be to be kind to others, as you are, Catherine."

Friday, December 17, 1830

Cassie and I this afternoon selected one of my mother's quilts—one with plenty of warmth in it yet tho' some parts worn and faded. This would be our answer to the fugitive's appeal. (Could he have known when he wrote in my book that I, tho' a child, had been installed in my mother's place? If so, were he a local man? Did Providence guide his hand?) Folding the quilt as small as we might, & wrapping some sausage and apples within, we crossed behind the Shipmans' house, reached the road, and thence proceeded to the phantom's stone. (Asa dubbed it thus one day, and the name has taken.)

As part of our plan I carried along the fateful lesson book. Should we be seen, or questioned, by neighbours I was well rehearsed to say that I was in search of a certain tree which I intended sketching. Cassie had come to companion me; and see, she carried a worn-out quilt should we become too cold. A pat excuse, we all believed, to fit the situation. A second purpose might be served by taking the book in hand: should we meet the stranger himself he'd know our purpose instantly; thus would not, likely, harm us.

The woods, as ever, were still and cold; the only sound the clacking of branches as, frozen, they touched one another. Sketchbook or no we did not tarry and tho' we saw no human sign, sped about our errand.

I turned but once as we left the spot where A. had discovered the fugitive's prints and which he'd occasioned to show to me along with a fire's remains. Of this I shall remember forever the look of that cold & wintry clearing, the quilt tucked in the foot of a tree & folded carefully to display a patch of brightest scarlet. I meant it also as a greeting—a flash of colour, a bit of warmth; the only thing man made, or brought, to that desolation.

Asa was at the gate. "Did you do it," he asked, low-voiced. "Yes," we said; and all of a sudden hot tears over-flowed. Again I saw that patch of scarlet and remembered my mother's voice, as she told her stories. "That grey," she'd said, "was a waistcoat once, the drab's my father's trousers. 'Tis said the pieces of scarlet are old, cut from the back of a Hessian's coat left behind in battle . . ."

"There, there, Cath," said Asa at last. Then he shifted from foot to foot, reached out for the edge of my cloak, and with it, wiped my cheek.

Saturday, December 18, 1830

The bread today was over-baked; the beans were barely softened. "Who loves you now?" teazed Father. (If he but knew the real, true cause of my present distraction!)

Monday, December 20, 1830

No more can I take my mind from the phantom than dare to re-enter the woods. Yesterday when a tree burst open, the cold and frost being very severe, the explosive sound set my heart to pounding—so certain was I the report was a rifle's, and my phantom discovered.

# ❧ V ❧

Thursday, December 23, 1830

We hear that even Winnipissogga is now frozen over. On our pond each afternoon the older boys gather after school to try their skill at skating. They boast that when they are dry and thirsty they only kneel at the edge of the ice and there find water to drink. These occur at the Northern part where underground streams flow through the Winter and run in to the lake. 'Tis icy water, and clear—

I told Father of their sport and that I thought it foolishness to skate there where the ice is thin, risking, likely, life and limb to slake a simple thirst. He only laughed and rumpled my hair. "There now, miss, I did the same and lived to tell about it." I think he'd not make light of it were I to be the skater.

Friday, December 24, 1830

When I came down to the kitchen this morning I discovered the following, deftly penned by Father:

> It requires but little discernment to discover the imperfections of others; but much humility to acknowledge our own.

Under it, ever so lightly sketched, the figure of a skater disported; and the initials, C.H., which are both Father's and mine.

Saturday, December 25, 1830

We attended services, this being Christmas Day. Can there, I wonder, be a chill more fierce than that which gathers in a building all week, then hurls itself, as if too long caged, at those who venture in. Although we wore our heaviest clothing it availed us not. The wooden pews gave forth great chill and the flooring, tightly laid, creaked when we walked across it. 'Tis much like a Winter Sabbath misplaced, and Sabbath it is tomorrow!

Later, our father read from the Bible as he often does. When it came time to prepare our meal Matty helped me to set things out: a loaf of bread baked yesterday, mugs of cyder, and our own good soup which I made in November, and we've had frozen in the buttery for these Winter days. So we dined most plentifully; grateful for the warmth of home, all mindful of the newborn babe born in Bethlehem long ago and the sweet young mother.

Monday, December 27, 1830

I was startled to think, this morning, I saw my phantom again! This time it proved a phantom phantom!—an upright stump seen through flung snow, revealed as being naught but that when the wind subsided!

Asa promises, the first he can, that he will venture in to the woods to see if the quilt be taken. There have been, these two weeks past, reports of modest thefts. A chicken here, some dried roots there, the largest of the Shipman pies. We presume this the work of our phantom, and do not speak of it.

Once I asked Asa about his thrashing and had it been very painful? "Skin soon cools," he said with a shrug, "and I had rather accept a beating than, by my denial, risk another's life."

Wednesday, December 29, 1830

The quilt we left for the phantom is gone; likewise the trail of foot prints, and every other sign. So said Asa yesterday, after he went to the woods. He thinks the prints to have been erased—mayhap with a log or stone—but certain it is that care was taken, and that the stranger is gone.

With Asa's words I felt released, even as if my feet would fly which have been heavily freighted during these past weeks.

Then I thought of he who must travel, slowly over frozen ground, and in unknown land.

"May he enjoy safe transport," I pray'd, "a safe end to his journey."

Saturday, January 1, 1831

A fair day, sparkling and bright—the first of this New Year. The snow has drifted in the yard out front, and sun and cold conspire together to make a glistening crust. In other years we have had more snow. But seldom is it so cold.

"Turn about and each in turn! Now you shall watch and I shall cook and here's to the evening meal." Thus Father announced a holiday in the New Year's honour!

How it regaled us, Matty and I, to watch his hands, so used to the plow, curve to women's implements and awkwardly employ them.

After we ate I took up my writing, and tho' I encouraged M. to knit she now lies curled on the settle, neither at work nor sleeping. She does not like to go up alone, especially when 'tis dark. So she avoids it, waiting in this way until I close my book. Then, together, we'll climb the stairs, first bidding Father a soft good night; and well I know, as we kneel to our prayers—saying them fast for the floor is cold!—we shall hear him here below, covering the fire against the back log, and always the last to bed.

Monday, January 3, 1831

Teacher Holt, in school today, read from the *newspaper!*

Wednesday, January 5, 1831

A spoon broke in my hand this morning. There are six, now, to be remolded, and scarcely as many whole. The tinker will have much work when he comes. Winter is hardly halfway through; already I long for its close.

Thursday, January 6, 1831

Snowed last night. It is fully up to the sills in front and well over that at the back of the house where the wind blows up from the hill. To keep the path to the barn door clear is the greatest struggle! Father says he some times wishes they'd set the buildings closer.

"I would have, too, were it up to me. But your mother was all against it. It wouldn't have been so pretty, she thought, nor taken advantage of the granite ledge before the centre door."

Once he said, "She had a way with her! A small, little thing to look at her. But she mostly got her way."

That is so hard to imagine—the days before I ever was born; Mother and Father were young then, so happy, & laughing in their pleasure.

# ❧VI❧

Friday, January 7, 1831

Cassie, Asa, Matty, and I walked home from school together. He loudly lamented the great injustice that he must struggle with Arithmetic while Cassie and I, indeed all we girls, are excused by reason of our Sex from all but the simplest cyphering, and the first four rules.

We hoped to go sledding after. But Mr. Shipman had need of Asa, and too soon it was dark.

Monday, January 10, 1831

Last week the teacher read from the paper; today he set no text! Instead, to improve our penmanship, he bade us each to practice upon lines of our own choosing.

"The idle Fool, Is whipt at School," was Asa's, occasioning laughter. Cassie undertook as hers: "Sudden and violent passions are seldom durable." I chose: "Better is a neighbour that is near, than a brother far off" (Proverbs XXVI, 10). Although I chose it to honour Cassie, all the while I worked at it, my mind was with the phantom. Indeed, it seemed a part of me travelled with him, across white fields, and toward what destination? "No, I must stay!" I imagined I cried; but was answered only by the soughing wind.

Thursday, January 13, 1831

Heavy snow these past three days; we are much confined to the house. Today there is so much wind and drifting we scarce can see the barn! Only the tops of the fence-posts show, each one domed with caps of snow, funny and misshapen. Until the road is broken out, for which we must wait till the storm is spent, school will not re-open. Although there is always work to do, yet is it of a different sort. 'Tis *half* a holiday.

Today I turned a shirt for Father & instructed Matty in how to turn a heel. I have shown her this before but she did not remember. Father, for his part, brought in some wood, nicely seasoned and matched as to grain, with some pieces partially carved. When I inquired what he would make he said he had gotten to thinking about a chair he started years ago. " 'Twas for your Mother, before she took sick"—and never had completed.

Friday, January 14

At mid-day today the storm let up; by dusk a few pale shadows appeared on the hillock'd snow. Father expects that tomorrow will be the day of the breaking out. This time we may go with him if the weather's not too severe!

Monday, January 17, 1831

This morning we dressed as warm as we might, turning ourselves into fat, funny bundles Aunt Lucy would not approve. I had on two dresses and a woolen underskirt, topped this with two shirts of *Father's*, and finally my shawl. Matty complained she could not bend her arms so thickly layered were her clothes and—"Cath-er-ine, it itches!"

"Better itch than freeze," I said. And scratched the frost from a window pane that we might observe the road. The house itself was nearly as cold as it was outdoors. We'd hardly wakened the fire this morning—only enough to prepare our meal—and now it was already banked to stay till our return.

Father had made his way to the barn, re-digging the path as he must each day against the swelling drifts. There he'd readied the oxen up and brought them out to wait in the yard—the yard itself reduced by snow with only as much of it cleared each day as we might need to use.

This morning the team breathed out great clouds. Father, to benefit by their warmth, placed himself between their bodies, but even so kept moving—it was that cold.

Because it hovered over them we saw the breath of approaching teams before the teams or drivers. Then, at last, they hove in sight. The men, deployed on either side, cast up shovelsful as they walked—tossing up snow to cap the drifts, whereby the spray and drift of snow was nearly continual. Behind them sparkled the marble-white road, no one's smirch upon it yet; the bed and banks were the same pure white. A dazzlement to the eye!

We saw six teams already in place, Mr. Shipman's being the last. Four more teams were yet to come. With us behind Mr. Shipman there'd be eleven teams. Twenty-two oxen! More than that in men!

We thought we might be to Holderness first, but were chagrinned on reaching the bridge that others were there before us.

Good-naturedly they teazed and joked: "Been sleeping, sugaring, or shovelling?" And what the answer may have been was lost amidst the laughter, and quick new round of jests.

Each of the taverns soon over-flowed. For if we were not the first to arrive, neither were we the last! From every hill by every road came lines of teams and men. The farthest to come was from College Road; the nearest from Shepard's Hill. Our own line of Coxboro men was neither near nor far. Matty first spotted our Uncle Jack—our frequent guest in Summer months but whom we see less often in Winter, the travel being harder and the days so early dark.

Uncle Jack calls the breaking out the closest a New-Hampshire Winter gets to the Fourth of July!

Once this day I feared Matty was lost. But there she came, soon enough, led by a cheerful if tipsy stranger saying cheerfully (to me!), "Here's your little one, ma'am."

We stayed till it was long after noon. The way home

lying mostly uphill we had a leisurely journey of it—taking our pleasure in the newly cleared road and telling each other the news we'd gleaned during our hours in town.

It was nearly dusk when we reached the house and very cold within. Father brought the fire to life, then went out and with his ax hacked off some of our frozen soup that we might start it heating while he attended to chores.

A knock at the door told of guests unexpected! It was no other than Teacher Holt who'd stayed behind with this and that and now was caught in the on-coming dark and still far from his lodgings.

Back went Father, with his ax, and soon returned to fill the pot which was quickly bubbling. As pleasant vapors filled the room I deemed myself amply rewarded for the slow preparation all those weeks ago! To the soup we joined bread and cyder, also nuts and apples. To offset the *plainness* of the food when we had a visitor I set out the pewterware and not the wooden bowls.

Teacher Holt talks with Father now and will stay the night. We have no proper chamber for guests, but he assures us he'll sleep well downstairs by the fire.

# ❧VII❧

Monday, January 24, 1831

You would never think how many people live in our State of New-Hampshire! Two hundred and sixty-nine thousand, five hundred and thirty-three!

Teacher Holt this morning showed us the *Columbian Centinel* for January the 8th. His friend, a Mr. Garrison, had sent it on from Boston.

Other true facts concerning our State:

> . . . increase in the last ten years, 25,372. The number of white males is 131,899, females 137,511; and of free coloured persons 623. The number of white persons deaf and dumb is 136 . . . and of blind 117.

How would it be, being blind? Cassie & I talked of this, closing our eyes to effect the condition as we walked homeward today. For all that we stumbled & clung to each other each of us knew, and knew full well, that we could open our eyes and *see* should we but choose to do so.

Thus we determined 'tis not solely the condition, but whether or not one has a choice that determines its oppression.

Then how would it be to be coloured? a slave? I proposed it might compare with perfect obedience. But no, says Cassie, obedience is free for the more *freely* one submits the better one obeys.

More than six hundred free coloured in New-Hampshire? I had not thought so many! With my phantom, should he be here still, there would be one more in number.

In all of these United States there are now 13 million people, some in each of the twenty-four states, but most in the Eastern Cities of Boston, Philadelphia, and New-York.

Thursday, February 10, 1831

Have not written in some days being chilled & feverish by turns, the latter now abating. Neither have I attended school but Cassie comes by daily and I have well employed the time with penmanship & spelling.

Matty is eight years old today, a sweet and trusting child. I can not but wish that Mother might see her—M. was so little when our mother died; nor does she remember the infant boy whom we called Nathaniel whose life was counted in days.

Father rejoiced so at his birth; every farmer needs a son and girls he already had. 'Twas funny to hear him talk to the infant who lay all swaddled and with no knowing of who it was that spoke to him nor the words' intention. I remember he talked to the child as if he were fully sensible. Once he promised he'd give to him—had indeed been saving for him—the Barlow knife that he, our father, had had when but a boy. I must have looked quite startled at this for Mother quickly interposed, "But not till he is nearly a youth—now, Charlie, don't be impatient for things that have to come with time." I think I remember this so well because soon after both sickened and died. And then there was no time.

Thursday, February 17, 1831

Teacher Holt brought in to school a copy of a newspaper started this month in Boston by his Boston friend. Mr. Garrison intends that his paper which he calls *The Liberator* will quite largely concern itself with the slavery question.

"Our country is the world," is its motto; "our countrymen all mankind."

Teacher Holt read the motto very plain, and later set it out in chalk, we to copy it in to our books and preserve it in our minds. Also he bade us consider a poem (It was printed in the newspaper.) whose author stated he'd rather be enslaved than knowingly allow cruel chains to deprive another. I thought of Asa, whipped for the pies. I could not see him where he sat, nor did he speak.

Friday, February 18, 1831

Cassie was not at school today, nor was Sophy Perkins. I and Asa and Matty walked home, and all the while it was on my mind to speak my admiration for what A. had done. Soon—too soon—we reached his gate and I had not spoken. Me to be shy with Asa Shipman! He whom I've played with like a brother, and who in deed *is* to me a brother, and closer to me in some ways than he is to Cassie . . .

Father has laid by much good cloth which he's woven these Winter months from yarn I spun last Summer. Because of this, and rebuilding the harrow which suffers with our rocky soil, he has had to neglect the chair with its delicate spindles. Despite this he plans a candle-stand: "We've been too long with no new things! A man, if he's not careful, finds that he has gotten stuck in his ways who never meant to be so. Yes, a chair *and* a candle-stand to stand by the North window there, with a cheery rug beside it. How would you like that, Catherine, my girl? But who will make the rug?"

Then off he went with some olden song with hums and words and whistles.

Had he (I think not.) expected reply? What would he have had me to say?

Sunday, February 20, 1831

Some of the district are sorely distressed that Teacher Holt has brought Boston's news into the school house hours. "Reading, writing, and cyphering," they say, "is all he's paid to know about; and all he ought to teach."

Behind this runs a darker rumour—one which strikes me with a dread I may not confess. Others had, it now appears, noted the foot prints in Piper's wood and harboured their suspicions. Now they believe, putting all together, that Teacher Holt had been the one to help the run-away! How easily we could clear his name but all of us fear to do so. O! there is no *end* to it; and tho' the phantom is long since gone, still does something of him remain. As alien it is, and unalterable, as the writing in my book and its plea, now answered.

Tuesday, February 22, 1831

Uncle Jack to visit. This is the first we have seen him since the breaking out. He too has heard the buzzing rumours about our Teacher Holt. Both he & Father oppose slaveholding, but have different ends in view. Father favours re-settlement, which would be in Africa and a new-formed nation. Uncle Jack says that freeman means free; as free as any man.

"But would you want, then," Father persists, "to have a black man as your neighbour, or thinking he might expect a share in the town decisions?"

Please miss.

Take pity.

I am cold.

Wednesday, February 23, 1831

As if he would do it in the town's despite, Teacher Holt has brought Boston's news into the school house to consider an advertizement which had appeared in a Southern newspaper. Mr. Garrison re-published it to call smug Yankee attention to the nature of the offenses which the South condones.

FOR SALE

A black girl, 17 years of age of excellent character, and of good disposition; a very useful and handy person in a house for a turn of years. Apply at the office of . . .

Seventeen years is scarcely older than the oldest at school. Suppose that we had been made to be slaves rather than being born free. Would not a black girl know love and fear—love and honour her father and mother, and fear lest anything change? I had not considered the matter in this way before.

The paper is dated the 5th of February. I wonder what befell her, where she may be now.

### Dialogue Between Youth, Christ, And the Devil

Awake, arise, behold thou hast
Thy life, a leaf, thy breath, a blast;
At night lie down prepared to have
Thy sleep, thy death, thy bed, thy grave.

(From our speller, page 36)

*Copy of letter submitted to the District Meeting by our Teacher. Shown to me by Cassie Shipman, who had it from her father, a Town Selectman this year.*

Neighbours, Friends, Employers:

Two issues are before us as I am doubly accused. First it is said that I have assisted an escaped *Negro slave* presumed to have been refuged in these, our nearby, woods. Second it is said that I have infringed upon my pupils' education by introducing, *in school hours*, texts other than school books, including newspapers.

Concerning the first my sole, only confession is that I have *not done* the thing of which I am accused. In this instance I would proudly accept that action's consequences. However, whatever his manner may suggest, or his dreams encourage, your school teacher is no conspirator, of that you may be certain.

Of the second complaint, I am guilty as charged, and pledge that I will desist. Whatsoever I did I did in good faith, believing my offices as a Teacher to include duties of Moral Education; that in a nation founded in Freedom, the Liberty of every man ought to be tested, assessed, & debated in every age, and decade, of that nation's life.

To so engage your children is not, however, your choice. As I am here by your let and permission, I truly regret the dissatisfaction that has been incurred. Mindful of my obligations, I beg you allow me remain in good faith,

Yr. Obdt. Servant,
E. Edw. Holt

# ❧VIII❧

Saturday, February 26, 1831

Saying it takes one's mind from the cold Cassie's mother says *every* Winter would be improved by such a *dispute*—and *nearly* each Winter has one. "A *heated* argument?" asks Cassie's father, and winks at that, 'midst merriment, which rather concludes the discussion.

Now must the teacher look for new lodging, the M.'s being loudest and first to condemn him, and where he is living besides! The Shipmans have offered to take him in. However, they (Shipmans) demand to be payed. The M.'s point out they've defaulted not and thus deserve the full fee for the unexpired term.

Father says this poor nation of ours can scarce expect its affairs in order so long as New-Englanders, being what they are, care more for cash than scruples.


Sunday, February 27, 1831

Teacher Holt sat with the Shipmans at services today.

Father says that when he is done with the spindled maple wood chair he'll *not* make a candle-stand after all, but rather another matching chair to keep it company. "Would not a chair want that," he jokes, "same as a mortal being?"

Tuesday, March 1, 1831

A delegation came 'round to the Shipmans and now the matter of Teacher Holt is as good as settled. Hereafter, in school, we'll read only such texts as the town approves. The M.'s will receive one half the due board, the rest of it going to Shipmans. As this leaves the Shipmans some dollars short, the teacher has pledged to Cassie's father that he shall work so and so many days come time for plowing and planting to satisfy the debt.

The Shipmans are well pleased. What farmer's household needs not more help, and some cash besides? 'Tis certain they have more chambers than they use despite Aunt Lucy's visit.

I had the wish Teacher Holt might come to us. This was not proposed.

The sun, I think, has acquired some warmth. Now when it filters through trees, still bare, it pits the snow beneath. Cassie says she saw two robins—the very first of the season. Tradition has it that luck will be hers. But Spring, I think, suffices; and Spring comes to us all.


Wednesday, March 9, 1831

> How welcome is the pretty bird
> Who sits upon the tree;
> Nor would I ask for gold or ~~silver~~ silk
> As Spring is wealth for me.

> C.C.H.

· 49 ·

Friday, March 11, 1831

Joshua Nelson was thrashed again for sleeping over his books. I know that I should die of shame; but he will ever make light of it, and grins when it is over.

"So what does it serve," I challenged Cassie. "Those who fear it avoid the lash; while those who mind not, mind not!"

We some times consider that we will be teachers, if only in the Summer months when females are employed. My mother was a teacher before she married. She used to tell how she met my father, being boarded at a farm near his, and much preferring his company to that of the cruder household at which she was lodged by the town.

Saturday, March 12, 1831

Father today completed his chair—a very excellent piece! One can tell it was made with care, and no part of it hurried. We set it in the Northeast window—there it will catch the sun in the morning, yet be at the margin of the light cast by the fire at night.

Matty begged to be the first person ever to sit in it! This she was allowed. As she placed her foot on the rung—a place where no foot had rested before—it came to me that one day the wood must be *worn away* from the smooth perfection of its present shape.

Yesterday I neglected to record what happened when I returned to the school house after the general dismissal.

Teacher Holt was at his desk and, sitting at the small scholars' benches, as if it were quite the usual thing, was a good half dozen of the older boys! Asa and David Shipman were there, and one of the older Prestons. Altho' one would scarcely know it was he, there I glimpsed Josh Nelson. Now he sat at full attention, his long knees bent to the low front bench, his chin cupped by his hands. Teacher Holt was in mid-discourse, Garrison's paper open. Catching sight of me he paused, asked if he might be of help, and then without a blush of shame, resumed his exhortation.

Cassie, when I told her of it, said that every one knows but me, and how had it escaped me? Teacher Holt abides by his promise not to teach, within *school hours*, texts not approved by the district. But *after* school is a different case, or so he reasons it out. Thus is the letter of the promise obeyed, while in their *spirit* the man and his scruples are not compromised! The district mayn't like it but there's naught that they can do.

Thursday, March 17, 1831

The sap, they say, is running in the better sheltered trees. No sooner had the word come 'round, none of ours being so favoured yet, than we must fetch the buckets out for scalding for new use. I think there was never a gladder sight, or a more certain sign of Spring, than pails uptilted to the sun on the South side of the house.

Although yard and road are boggy in places, yet in the deeper part of the woods is there a foot of snow. 'Tis there they will take the oxen tomorrow, their very passage with drag-logs behind serving to clear a path to the camp where we'll have the sugaring off.

Friday, March 18, 1831

Today I am fourteen years old!

While I prepared our mid-day dinner Father came to talk about the day that I was born. He remembers well it had snowed *nine inches* just the night before my birth, and ten the day preceding. Most of the previous snow had melted and they'd had flooding on River Street down in Holderness. The sun's first rays came in to the room as I came in to the world. They'd wrapped me well and there, with my mother, I lay in the room which they'd planned for the purpose and called the borning room.

(Later my mother died in that room, but none ever called it a dying room that I heard tell about. I do not like to think of it—her face that had gone on a sudden old, and all its colour gone.)

Father, this morning, was full of good cheer & told how proud and happy they'd been, the house being newly completed and now graced with a child.

He had three acres mowing, he says, and half a one

arable. One each of horse, & cow, and ox—the latter my mother had nursed to health when no one else was able. (The horse died just before she did. Was injured, sickened, up & died. We never got another.)

The whole first year they had only a table, some benches my mother had brought from her home, and a pot for cooking.

Saturday, March 19, 1831

Today the men went in to the woods to tap the trees and hang the buckets which we had readied by sunning and scalding and then had loaded on to the cart for transport to the camp.

We, Matty and I and the Shipman children, assisted as we might. (Little Willie was excluded from this being still too small to go to the woods, to his great disappointment.) Even as the taps were placed—the men doing this throughout the grove—the boys cut pine boughs which we then used to re-cover the shanty. They expect to start the fires tomorrow when the Sabbath ends. ('Tis is a well-known New-England tradition, sprung from a mountainous land: start the Sabbath by the almanac, but end it when the Western hills first lay claim to the sun. Thus are the Saturday hours prolonged while the desired reverse effect is applied to the Sabbath's duration.)

# ❧IX❧

Monday, March 21, 1831

Although, in memory, sap runs fast the *actual* accumulation is drop by drop, and slow. Hardly any attended school; all help is needed that can be had to feed the fires and stir the kettles and join the speculation: will it soon turn sirup?

Tonight our father will stay at the camp to keep the fires going.

Tuesday, March 22, 1831

Father says 'twas grand! Many friends and neighbours came out, and Sophy's father, Mr. Perkins, was there, and had brought his fiddle! For nourishment there was the sirup itself. One tastes it carefully with sipping spoon, or ladles some off—preserving the boil—to pour on the clean white snow. The sudden chilling brings a thick waxy sugar, which is every one's treat.

Father says Cassie's brother, David, gave his dog a great thick lump which sealed the poor dog's jaws. So he could neither chew nor bark—both of which he now longed to do—till it had dissolved away.

A rather bad accident has befallen Joshua Nelson's mother. He tells that her cow raised its head up quick, thereby sticking a horn through her cheek & knocking her out completely. No one else was there at the time. So she took care of herself. Joshua says she's mending nicely. Mrs. Shipman, on hearing what happened, sent 'round some new baked loaves of bread, and the last Thanksgiving pie.

Thursday, March 24, 1831

Warm, cold, and once again warm. There is consternation here lest the warmer weather bring an early end to the sap.

Concerning the seasons Father observes 'tis very nearly the same as with the seasons of men's lives. The baby not only crawls and creeps, but walks a step or two—and falls—and then 'tis many weeks or months before the true achievement. The aging grandad sinks so low the family thinks him gone. Then is the oldster up and about, spry and bright as you please. But this time is his time well run. So when the next decline occurs, it carries him to the grave. "And you, my girl," says Father to me, pressing his hands against his knees and rising from his chair, "you've been a woman while yet a child . . . Well, we shall see if Time or contrivance restore sweet youth to you."

A chill passed over me at that. I yearned to protest that I was happy, would have it no other way. Something in his manner bade me hold my tongue.

Friday, March 25, 1831

> Let thy speech be better than silence, or be
> silent.
>
> Dionysius, the Elder

*Mrs. Shipman's Receipt for Mince Meat:*

A pound of meat, suet, sugar, raisins,
currents, *each*—6 large pippin apples, ¼ lb.
citron, 1 oz. of cinnamon, 1 oz. of cloves,
the same of nutmeg—a quart of brandy and
a quart of wine.

Sunday, March 27, 1831

As feared, the sugaring was halted early by the quirky
weather. That is ever the farmer's lot, who must be grateful when Fortune smiles, resigned when she turns away.

It is good that a new & lively *topic* is offered for con-
versation! Indeed I think it fair to say that no one talks of
any thing else. Truly is Priest Fowle's sermon forgotten in
this occurrence! This Tuesday past as we have learned, an
elegantly appointed coach appeared in Meredith. It bore
but a single passenger, a gentleman in foreign dress who
asked in perfect English, whether a Mr. Jeremy Preston
still lived thereabouts; that is Sophy's grandad's brother on
her mother's side. On being told Mr. Preston's location,
the stranger said he had business with him, but would not
reveal its nature.

By nightfall every one knew!

It happened that many years ago a Reverend Williams bound out his youngest son to the merchant Preston. One night the boy returned late to his lodging, he having spent the evening in the company of *girls*. For this offense he was whipped next day, as was to be expected.

Nevertheless, the next night he ran off, taking with him some three hundred dollars from his employer's desk! The theft was discovered with the boy's escape, & he was traced to Portsmouth. There his pursuers were utterly foiled; he had signed on with a Russian ship and she had sailed that morning. Two dockside lads who'd helped put her out remembered the farm boy well.

As has now been learned hereabouts, pirates attacked when the ship was mid-ocean and the youth became a hero! For but for his wit, and courage too, the frigate would have been over-run and all its men taken captive. Upon arrival in St. Petersburg, the boy was made very much of indeed, and soon presented—his grace and charm exceeding!—to the Czar himself! In time he was made a nobleman, and not too long thereafter, an admiral in the navy.

Through all these years he kept his secret, it pricking him from time to time as a thorn or sliver will if it be not removed. So when, in connection with his business affairs, a Boston visit must be arranged, the one-time runaway lad resolved he would seek out the place of his indenture, his unhappy origins, and his youthful offense.

Thus did he travel to Meredith in the hired coach. When, resplendent, he stood before the humble man whose service he'd escaped, the stranger announced most ringingly, "I, sir, am Count Zincheroff, of St. Petersburg."

"Beg pardon, and I know you not," the bewildered merchant replied.

"Then do you remember a boy named Williams to whom you gave a thrashing and who then disappeared? He took three hundred dollars too. No doubt you remember that!"

At this the old man remembered him well, but could make no sense of it all. But now the Count took out his purse, and asked the extent of the debt.

"The extent of the debt, sir? Why, as you've said! 'Tis but the three hundred dollars that you took from me."

But remarking that had it lain in a bank the money would have increased in time, he payed it all in golden coin—how it glinted in the sun according to those who were there! Then he addressed the curious crowd: "Now, my countrymen, for so you are still, I go back to Russia, as an honest man!"

Having thus fulfilled his obligation he had no desire to tarry. He quickly stepped in to the waiting coach & soon was out of sight.

I scarce can believe this marvellous tale! Today the words are on every tongue: The Count of Meredith!


Monday, March 28, 1831

Joshua saw it, and he told Asa, and Asa told Cassie and me: Teacher Holt and Aunt Lucy kissed, sitting together, 'round the fire, at the sugaring off.

Wednesday, March 30, 1831

I was the winner at spelling today bringing down Joshua Nelson with ac-com-pan-y. I think his mind was not on it tho'—his error was such a foolish one, to neglect to double the "c."

He took his defeat in excellent humour and even told me, "Fairly won!" when we met after school.

April Fool's Day, 1831!

Matty and I played a great prank on our father this morning. Yesterday, on conceiving the trick, I pared down a firm white turnip to resemble the end of a candle. After we all had retired last night, and making sure he preceded us in sleep, we tiptoed down and, with our "candle," replaced the one he uses daily to start the morning fire.

As soon as we heard a noise below—we'd scarcely slept a wink all night for fear that we should miss it—Matty and I wrapped up in quilts and crept to the foot of the stair.

He applied the flint for the longest time. But the "candle" would not burn. It happened that the early dark helped preserve our secret. Altho' he peered at it several times he did not detect the replacement! Now indeed did he lose his temper, calling on spirits of every sort, and cursing the damp of a Spring-time morning which made the wick—or *so he thought*—so stubborn and *refractory* to the flint's persuasion.

Of course, in time, he took hold of the thing and then the sport was out. We were helpless before our laughter; and tho', at first, he pretended wrath he quite soon joined in.

"The best prank ever," he then pronounced and added with mock severity, "But next time thrashing awaits such sisters as make the father the fool!"

Monday, April 4, 1831

This morning I had Matt put on a dress she's not worn for a season. Her poor little hands and wrists stuck out, and Father said he guessed he got *two* young ladies now.

Now nothing will do but we have new clothes, and I suppose we must. Father will fetch the yard goods home when he goes back to Boston. Already in the Concord paper the local merchants advertize dress goods of summer weight.

I faithfully mend whatever I can; nor am I ashamed to wear a garment when the patch is neatly done, the collar nicely turned.

Yet now that he's put the thought in my head I think of nothing else! I've been so long without a new frock! I suppose Cassie's mother will say of the cloth, "Remember, Charles, that blue shows soil and would not homespun do?" But O! I would love a darling blue dress all cut to the latest fashion.

# ❧ X ❧

Tuesday, April 5, 1831

Scarcely a dozen of good apples left, and fewer still of cabbage! The larger potatoes are sprouting again! However, as this is the third time around, it will be the last time if I catch them quick enough. Parsnips, of course, are now at their best. I use them often, mashed and plain, or cook them into soup.

Thursday, April 7, 1831

"Cath," says Asa, "will you help me out? And promise you'll not tell Cassie? I'm bound to give this verse to Sophy, and blamed if I can do it—"

He means it for the last day of school when custom dictates the exchange of keepsakes—verses, love knots, locks of hair—that the receivers may know, and preserve, the tender emotions of the donors over the Summer months.

The verse as he'd attempted it was crammed on a scrap of paper. Folded and overwritten it was, as if its author had mightily striven over the lines he shewed me:

Summer's but a season,
October's gold a leaf;
Prayer quickly vanishes
Heavenward and brief.
Random are the gestures
~~O'er~~ Towards me you have flung

"All I can think of is stung, and sung. And neither fits," he finished.

"Wrung?" I offered, "as wrung out a shirt? Or rung —as for bells? Or the rung of a chair—"

At this he warned me not to teaze, threatened he'd never speak to me more if I persisted in it.

Said I quickly, "I teaze you not," tho' of course I did. Then I thought a moment, and offered him new lines:

Random are the little words
To me you have spoken;
But the promise I make you now
Never shall be broken.

"*What* promise, Cath?" he asked me, vexed. "I swear you're making no sense at all. Come now, you can do it."

So then I knew how it was with him, and set to rhyming one line and another, none of which wholly pleased him. Then back we came 'round to where we'd begun, as so often happens.

Random are the gestures
With which you've won my heart;
Yet for all the days to come
May we never part.

He copied it down and hurried off, the paper shoved firmly into a pocket, which threatened to reduce it to shreds, as its predecessor. Just at the rise he shouted his thanks. Then he vaulted the wall at the property line, and struck out through the meadow, and by that means, to home.

Sophy's mother advises this receipt. She says it makes a successful cake, and easily prepared:

> One cup of butter, two cups of sugar, three cups of flour, and four eggs well beat together. It may be baked in pans or cups, no more than twenty minutes.

I intend to try it.

Wednesday, April 13, 1831

The closing day of school. Joshua gave me forget-me-nots. Where he found them I cannot think, it being very early. Attached by a ribbon was a small square of paper on which he had neatly written: "I pray you accompany me."

We all did nicely with the spelling matches, saying of pieces, and recitations—even the abcedarians left naught to be ashamed of and made many a parent proud. Over all of this our teacher presided—presided with a *flourish* I might say, as if he were *determined* to show that one might challenge his politics but never fault his teaching.

Asa presented his poem to Sophy, along with a

ribbon'd lock of hair which she accepted, smiling. I hope that neither one heard, as did I, some grandad in the back row say: "Give the lass a year or two and she's like to have enough of hair to stuff a fair sized pillow!"

After school, the day being mild, we did not hurry home. Asa proposed we cross through the woods. How different it looked—all dappled and warm—than it had done that Winter's day when Cassie and I came bearing our quilt to do an act of charity (or folly) for fugitive (or villain).

## Thursday, April 14, 1831

Mrs. Shipman considers *wasted* the day on which there is naught accomplished, and waste the worst of sins. Therefore were we three obliged—Cassie, Matty, and I together—on the *loveliest* day of Spring to each let down an outgrown frock and re-sew the hem. Cassie and I are held to the rule of twelve full stitches to the inch; Matty, younger, is spared. "Any work worth doing," recites Mrs. Shipman, "is worth doing well."

By the time I got up from the table my fingers were cramped, my neck was stiff, and indeed my whole back *ached* with the prolonged effort of bending over so close!

## Saturday, April 16, 1831

Father departs on Monday for Boston. There has been very much to do in that trip's preparation. Furs must be bundled—both his own and Mr. Shipman's—for these are principal among the things he will take to trade. Also, cut and packed in blocks, is maple sugar—the work of hours—to sweeten city palates. Topping the load are brooms of straw, still retaining their golden colour and some of Summer's fragrance.

These things will allow him for cash, or in trade, to obtain the next season's supplies: such foods and herbs as we can not grow, items for mending tools and the like, and parts for the larger contraptions required by the farm. Yard goods we cannot weave at home he will buy if the price is right, or an odd bolt strikes his fancy. Some times there is a book, or toy, or some pretty thing, or even sweets, if he's traded well.

Others in the district go to Concord to trade, it being so much nearer. But Father prefers Boston's greater choice, and claims he finds better trading for the items which he brings. It is all very much to arrange. He drives there Mr. Shipman's team—horses making better time—but as he must then also trade for them there is more to carry, coming and going back.

He will return in one week's time, all going well. Matty and I are to stay on here; Cassie's father will help with the stock as he has done before. As 'change work for this and the use of the team we're to give two days plowing when it comes time for that.


Monday, April 18, 1831

Father left this morning, long before it was light. This is to put the time to his journey, which is a long, dreary way with a wagon and no relief for the team; even the coach will take more than twenty hours for the usual run.

I packed for him some journey cake, also some pieces of hearty cheese, and the last of the Winter's apples. To-night, if he stops at an inn to sleep, he need not spend good money to obtain his food.

Matty and I both waved him off, she standing on the gate-post to follow him with her eyes. However, the dark-ness obscur'd his form even before the curving road took him from our sight. A few times more we glimpsed the lantern that swung from the wagon seat. After that there were some few sounds—the creak of wheels and the horses' bells—and when there was only silence we turned back to the house.

This morning I carried over to Shipmans' a good two baskets of clothes for washing—their kettles will hold both theirs *and* ours—and Cassie and I can work together, and each have company. The day being fair, with a wind for drying, I included bed sheets & casings that otherwise might have waited.

"But what does he *do?*" I questioned Cassie, speaking of Teacher Holt. Every one knows he's stayed on at the Shipmans'; tho' the term is long since ended.

The task we stood at allowed us to talk—better than on the days we sew—for we have only to tend the kettles and to keep the fires. I always find it quaint to see how shirts and trousers rise to the surface, the former waving their empty sleeves, and presently seeming to vanish beneath the sudsy, steaming waves. Soon we must wring the gar-ments out, turning the heavier pieces between us, and drop them in to a second kettle, there to continue the cleansing. But even while doing this we may talk; and talk, this day, we did!

"But what does he do?" I asked again, as the subject of my question walked across the yard.

"I hadn't noticed that he does *much*," Cassie said, sounding quite like her mother, "unless you count the time at courting—bundling with Aunt Lucy by night & mooning around by day!"

Sabbath-day, April 24, 1831

The week is wearisome and long. The house, without Father, is empty and still and Matty shadows my every step as an infant will.

Went to services both times with Shipmans; walked home with Cassie and Asa in the afternoon.

Monday, April 25, 1831

This being the day we expected Father we have not left the house. However, it is evening now and he has not come. I earnestly pray no harm has befallen the one on whom we so depend, and whom we hold so dear.

Tuesday, April 26, 1831

When again, today, we must tell ourselves that he would not come, I carried down to the cellar to keep the mince that I had made. (I used Mrs. Shipman's receipt, making only half the amount, as I had used it once before and Father pronounced it tasty.)

" 'Twill be as good tomorrow," I said.

"Better," said Matty loyally, which was good of her.

Thursday, April 28, 1831

With what joy we sighted the wagon, and sped down the road to meet him before he reached the yard. I and Matty had much to say, whereat he called us "Magpies, both!" and claimed to have the best news of all would we but let him tell it.

He is going to marry, he said! She is widowed, a Mistress Ann Higham, and has a son my age!

### Letter to me from Mistress Higham

(It was tucked in a bonnet for me which she had selected.)

My very dear Catherine,

May I call you so? I feel that I care for you very much, can only love you more.

The bonnet is blue, because of your eyes, of which your father told me.

I know I shall have much to learn; and pray you will be my help & friend, as I hope to be yours,

Ann Higham

Saturday, April 30, 1831

On Thursday evening the Shipmans were here; yesterday Uncle Jack. Mrs. Shipman is over-joyed that she'll soon have a neighbour woman, while Uncle Jack too roughly jokes he'll be the next to fall.

Father keeps telling the story over—"Went in to a shop to buy me some goods and found, instead, a wife!" Then he explains that the boy is named Daniel, and never had a father. The young husband died a scant two weeks before the son was born. In these difficult circumstances, and having herself and the babe to feed, Mistress Higham had *taken up* her brother's offer to board with him and help out in his shop. Her labour being exchanged for the lodging she hadn't felt beholden to him; and there she had stayed these twelve, thirteen, years; and there she had met my father.

Monday, May 2, 1831

A letter which Father received today confirms that they shall marry in Boston at the end of the month.

Is not late May an odd time for a wedding, with so much here that has to be done, and with Spring plowing and planting?

Joy and sorrow, says our father, each makes its own season.

# ☙XI☙

Friday, May 6, 1831

A Jew, a peddlar, came by today, the first Jew I have seen. His hair was long and his beard was scant, but it hung uncut. We did not ask him in to the house, but offered food and cyder to him, of which he took only the latter.

I bought of him some needles and buttons, also sewing silk. He had scissors for sale at 12¢ each and some for twice that amount. When I inquired the difference between, such amusement came in to his eyes his whole face was transformed!

"Well now, I'll tell you," he said with a smile, "and my compliments, miss!" Then he explained that when first on the road he sold his wares as cheap as he might so to increase his trade. But customers told of his prices believed he carried tawdry stuff. To put the principle to the test he made two packets of the self-same scissors, calling some "fine" and the others "good buys," and found that people preferred the more costly, supposing them to be better. Since then his goods are more dearly priced. "Except," he concluded merrily, "for someone with sharp eyes, like yourself!" And leaving me to ponder this statement he climbed up to his seat.

Such a curious fellow, and likeable in his candor. I hope when he comes by again he'll not neglect to call.

Saturday, May 7, 1831

I told Asa about the Jew. He was sorry he had not seen him.

Monday, May 9, 1831

Again a letter for Father from *her!* And Father makes no secret of it; he is as eager as a boy, and specially goes to the bridge on Mondays so as to be there when the mail's handed down from the Boston coach.

Her letters are neatly sealed and folded, and with a

well-schooled hand. Beside them my own look poor and untidy, hard tho' I may try.

Cassie, known to be delicate, is this week indisposed.

Tuesday, May 10, 1831

A new pine dresser was installed today, a large and handsome piece.

Using salt and vinegar, we rubbed the pewterware till it shone, then set it out on the dresser. If we'll not use it until she comes, it will retain its lustre, and such is my intent.

Father goes in two weeks' time. He is very hard pressed these days to put all in order. It came to me 'tis the very last time that this, our house, will be ours alone, not also hers, and Daniel's.

Friday, May 13, 1831

A cold rain, with grey skies, and chilly underfoot. Not much pleasure in bare feet today, especially as they are unaccustomed, after the leathern housing of Winter, to go about unprotected.

Matty hops from stone to stone, rubs one foot 'gainst the other one's leg, looking very like a cricket—and very streaked besides!

"I *have* to do it," she explains, sensing my disapproval.

"That's the way I get them warm, and—honest!—I'll wash myself!"

Father, at least, is pleased with the rain, well-timed before Spring planting.

Saturday, May 14, 1831

Father has had a jacket made lest he appear too rude a sort in city company.

"Will not your old one do," I asked, "the one you wore at Closing Day, and still put on for church?"

"Now, miss," he said, "we'll have none of your sulks, and none of your savings either. I tell you we are *fortunate* that Mistress Higham has accepted to make her home with us."

So the new jacket—sewn for a fee!—by a seamstress-woman in town. It is grey, as a sheep's wool is. The colour becomes him nicely. The stuff should wear very well, I think, it being closely woven.

Tuesday, May 17, 1831

"Shall I have need of this or that? Please ask Catherine if . . . ?" Yesterday's letter abounded with questions which Father read aloud. He seems not to think it odd that she should be so unknowing and so unashamed. " 'Tis good," he approves, "that she thinks to ask. How many others would? Come then, Catherine, what shall I say? Or do you prefer to prepare a reply that I may carry with me, it being of women's work?"

Even Cassie who is my friend is wont to take her side! "After all, Catherine," she enjoins. "It must be ever so *diff'rent* for her, living in Boston till now."


Wednesday, May 18, 1831

Father departed this morning. Again he drove the Shipmans' team, both to hasten the journey and better present himself. The wagon itself we washed with care and have recovered the seat. The case in which Father packed his clothes bulged with the new-made woolen jacket, a fine linen shirt (of Mr. Shipman's), and other items, his own and borrowed, that he will wear for the wedding itself or in the course of his stay.

Also in the back of the wagon were some brooms to be traded. "Might as well" and "No reason not!" They fetched an excellent price last month; he hopes they will do so again. Also he took more maple sugar, and for the same reason. (We do not generally trade two times. But Father's determined to make a fair impression on Mistress Higham's family, and will not appear before them without his pockets lined.)

He gave us each a kiss on parting. "Look after your sister," were his words to me; then quickly he mounted the wagon seat and adjusted the reins. I did my best to return his smile, and waved till he was gone.

Sunday, May 22, 1831

On this day, in Boston, they married. I will not call her Mother.

Thursday, May 26, 1831

She is less tall than I expected—smaller, even, than Mrs. Shipman; and plainer than Aunt Lucy.

Daniel, too, is plain. He, however, is rather tall, with a sprinkling of freckles, and none too large a jaw. Just below the crown of his head his hair sticks out in a little tuft. D. brushes it often, in nervous gesture, but this avails him not.

"Yes, sir," "No sir," and "Thank you, sir" were all he said today. 'Tis quite a different brother we've got than I had expected, knowing the Shipman boys.

Later

Soon, for the first time, when we go up to sleep, D. will go up with us. He will use the farther quarter, towards the Western side. Mr. Shipman and David this week helped carry up a new straw mattress and a roped bed frame. There is space alongside for a box of possessions such as D. may have thought to bring. Father, now that he is returned, says he'll gladly drive some pegs for Daniel to hang his clothes upon—as many as he'll need.

Matty stares and stares. Meeting up with me she whispered, "Did you see, Cath, did you see? He's got freckles *inside* his ears!"

Friday, May 27, 1831

Tho' I know full well they gawked at the windows when Father's wagon came up the road, the Shipmans waited until today before they made a call.

"We thought you might be tired a bit, from the exhaustion of the journey—and here, you see, we've brought you some pudding—'tis simple fare, but we're farmers here, but my sister, who is from Salem, enjoys it when she's here."

Alas for Mrs. Shipman! I know she'd awaited with eagerness her new neighbour's arrival. Yet she, on this occasion of meeting, was awkward and out of grace. Perhaps she feared the Boston woman would scorn her country ways.

But the Boston woman had worries of her own. "So very kind of you," she smiled. "The pudding will be delicious, I'm sure! Won't you please sit down? Here, let me draw up a chair for you; unless, of course, I didn't mean—well, perhaps, it *ought* to stay by the window's light?"

Our Father stood there, quite dispossess'd till, arriving later than the others, Aunt Lucy saved the day!

"I hear you've come from Boston," she said—as if they'd talked of anything else for the past two weeks! "Tell me," she said, "is it true about . . ." And all at once there were bursts of chatter; the ladies, at least, at ease.

Sabbath-day, May 29, 1831

All eyes turned when we entered the church. Father looked careful and very proud—again wore his new grey jacket. She seemed shy—as well she might—and kept her eyes cast down.

Daniel walked between me and Matty, looking straight ahead. People were curious, mostly kind. But when my ears caught someone's whisper—"She's hardly got the first one's looks"—I quickly hoped it escaped her hearing, although I think it true.

The day being mild we walked home slowly; Father talked gently all the while, as if to ease the awkwardness at being so much on view.

# ❧XII❧

Monday, May 30, 1831

Around us all is fresh new green; new grass, small flowers, new leaf. On such a day it is hard to recall the recent bogginess under foot, the heavy mud on the roads.

This morning we carried down armloads of bedding, Matty and I at her direction, to air in the fresh Spring sun.

Some, not having been used of late, gave off a musty smell.

Once she paused, looking out at the hills, and spoke so softly as to make me think I was not meant to hear: "Let me remember this thankful moment later, when I've doubts." Certainly it was a curious thing for a new wife to say. Another time, as she folded a quilt: "Such fine work here; and made for use! May I be proven worthy to carry on the task."

Tuesday, May 31, 1831

Talk started up about the Jew—who had seen him and who had not and from whence he came. Uncle Jack, who chanced to be here, said it put him in mind of a story which he then put to Father.

"A man there was who held that Italian was his favourite tongue. In argument with a Bible scholar, the latter preferring the Hebrew Language, the former was heard to remark:

" 'You can't deny that when God Almighty thrust poor Adam out of Eden he spake Hebrew to him.'

" 'That may be,' the scholar replied, 'But I take it as *certainty* that if God spake *Hebrew* when Adam was ejected, Eve was speaking *Italian* when Adam was seduced.' "

Father slapped his knee at this and, as if to recall his pleasure, repeated the final line.

Pleased by his story's great success Uncle Jack chuckled, winked, and said: "And they waste pupils' good time these days on the study of Greek?"

"Please," she said, compressing her lips, "there are children here."

She said no more, nor had to. Uncle Jack left soon thereafter, saying that he had "much to do," and firmly refusing our Father's entreaties to reconsider and stay. Afterwards Father fussed about, finally bursting forth to say, "You *know* he meant no offense!"

Wednesday, June 1, 1831

How different are the dresses she's brought from those of Cassie's mother. Yet freely she pegs an apron around them, puts a shawl atop them when chilled, and goes about as if unconcerned at her odd appearance. Open V's at throat and back, and well-shaped bodices tightly tucked, were never meant for farm work, or the country life.

Friday, June 3, 1831

Now are we busy from dawn to dusk with things she finds in need of doing, and all with our assistance! I think I have not seen Cassie to speak since she, & D., arrived.

The last of the bedding has been brought down, including the quilts my own mother brought when she came as a bride. I worry lest she should inquire why there are only eleven of these instead of the usual dozen. How little we knew when we put it out what was to befall.

Within the house we scrub and sweep. You would not think that before she came *I* had cleaned it well! This, it seems, is Spring Cleaning—and must be done from top to bottom whether 'tis needed or no. Today she enlisted Daniel's help to carry out (and in again) all the furnishings! Some of the pieces are assigned new places; the old planked table's drawn near the hearth, the fashion, she says, in Boston. She intends to hang it with a cloth, and set a lamp in the middle. The dresser's been moved to a farther wall—handier to the work of the kitchen in her estimation. Still does the new chair retain its place, and the settle's still by the fire.

Last night I sat there next to her while Father read from the Bible as he so likes to do. Daniel and Matty had been out of doors but came inside with darkness. Then joining together, five voices as one, we easily followed Father in prayer, and so retired to bed.

Tuesday, June 7, 1831

Cassie came by this morning to say I must come and see! They've a grand new mural along the stair, and in the parlour too! The latter is in the most popular style but was done in a single day! It shows a hillside, and farm, and elms; the latter, says Cassie, in tiny leaf, that it may be Spring for ever!

The stenciller showed me a book he had from which I copied out nearly a page for my future instruction.

The stencils are made from metal plates, there being one for every colour, and of each *part* of the design. The desired effect of landscape or scene is achieved by the muralist through their knowing combination. In this manner an entire scene may be readily constructed and far more quickly executed than by free-hand drawing.

*From* The Curious Arts *by one*
*Rufus Porter:*

> Every object must be painted larger or smaller according to the distance at which it is represented; thus the proper height of trees in the second distance is one to two inches, the other objects in proportion. Those in the first distance from six to ten inches generally; but those in the foreground, which are nearest, are frequently painted as large as the walls will admit. The colours also for distant objects, house, ships, etc., must be varied, being mixed with more or less sky blue, according to the distance of the object. By these means the view will apparently recede from the eye and will have a very striking effect.

"Very striking effect," indeed. I think I never till now have seen any murals as handsome as these. 'Tis hard to restrain my envy. But I largely succeeded, and confess'd it not.


Wednesday, June 8, 1831

The start of Summer school! Of our household & the Shipmans, I, Matty, and Cassie will go. Asa and David will help their father; Willie might go but that Mrs. Shipman is reluctant to give up her baby sooner than she must. Daniel, like the other boys, will be working the farm. Father notes this with quiet pride. I never thought, before this time, he might have minded that he must ever beg after help; thus wait until the others were done to commence his haying. We gladly helped him, Matty and I. But our strength was insufficient for some shares of the work.

At the school house we were met with exclamations, happy tears, and crying after news! Mary Nelson, Joshua's sister, has gone, we hear, to Tiltonboro for a Summer's teaching position. Sophy's uncle, her mother's younger brother, got a foot so badly mangled they had to cut it off. He is all right now.

Matty, this morning, was all impatience. And truly one *would not believe* that any pupil before this day had studied penmanship. Father gave her a new lead plummet which he had shaped himself. This implement dangles brightly from a new birch ruler, bought for *her*, by means of a flaxen string. Also from Father a sharpened quill; from *her* a pewter inkstand. I think this may have been her own when she was a girl. It bears the marks of frequent use, nor was it any of ours. She's promised, too, a new manuscript book—and tho' we have enough of plain paper at hand, *Matty's* copy-book is to be bound with patterned paper, sent from Boston, but not yet arrived.

The new teacher's name is Miss Orpha Williams. She is kind and tiny; hardly taller than I! I fear the larger of the boys, if such attend the school this Summer, will take advantage of her. She was to have come a week ago but was delayed in arrival. Thus is delayed also the opening day of school.

Thursday, June 9, 1831

I heard the clatter as I came up the road, coming home from school. The weaver! I thought. And so it was, earlier than in other years; but this is a different weaver than we've had before. She liked his looks, is all she said, and thought he was well-spoken. I would rather have waited for the one we know.

The loom's set up in the parlour already, and from its opened windows the clatter emanates.

He'll make a new coverlet for their bed—the dark blue pattern for the Winter months, and a lighter Summer side. 'Tis a rather old-fashioned pattern, but she prefers it still.

Friday, June 10, 1831

The truth is told about the quilt. It happened in this manner, and Matty was the cause:

With the weaver here these days there has been considerable talk of linens and bedding, sewing and quilts, quilting designs and their stories. Flying Geese? Moon over Mountain? Star of Bethlehem? She knows a host of them by name—both those she's made and otherwise —and likes to talk about them.

"Then *you* tell the story," says Matty to me, "about the red's from the Russian's coat, and grab the father's trousers."

"But what can you have in mind?" I asked, her words being so outlandish that they caught me unaware. Embarrassed by my answer to her Matty now shrilled at me: "The Russian's coat! You know it, Cath! And you and Cassie took the quilt and—"

"Matty!" I gasped, too late.

"Catherine," she queried, drawing a thread & smoothing down her stitching, "does the child mean yet *another* quilt, one I know not of?"

Until that moment no lie was asked, as I had reminded Cassie so many months ago. As for the deception itself, I'd long since found the justification in Teacher Holt's well-known remarks, and Uncle Jack's opinions.

But now I must tell the truth or lie, deny that Cassie and I had done what Matty had seen us do.

I blurted: " 'Twas anyway a very old quilt. You wouldn't have liked it at all!" Then red-faced and tearful I told it all. The missing book. The message found. Our hard-won decision and the precepts given in school. Even Asa's whipping and the stolen Shipman pies.

"Catherine, Catherine," was all she said. Then: "I'm so put to the test!" She made an attempt to resume the sewing but only snarled the thread. As for my part I could not speak & I remember nothing of Matty in this while.

"Come," she said, calm regained, and led us to the Summer kitchen to start the evening meal.

Halfway through that work she exclaimed, "And did you not think on the danger to you? What cruel misfortunes might have occurred, harm to you, or Cassie?"

"No," I said. "He was cold. And 'twas winter then."

"Dear child," she said, "for you *are* but a child . . ." Then she advanced as if to embrace me, but as soon withdrew. "Come," she said with an effort to be brisk. "I'm afraid we have fallen idle. Run, quick, Matty, and fetch us some water. Catherine, that fire needs wood. As for the quilt I must think on it; must search out what to do."


Early morning, Saturday, June 11, 1831

Last night I heard them talking. Mostly her voice; then Father's. They spoke so low the words were indistinct. Then her laugh rang out.

"But Charlie," she said, "it is really so funny! Grab the father's trousers!"

Then he chuckled, then murmurings; then were we all asleep.

Later Saturday

I am to make a replacing quilt. That she has decided &
our father agreed. When I protested I could do it not—that
I knew hemming, running, and felling, overstitch and but-
tonhole, but not to make a quilt—she smiled despite the
solemn moment, and my urgency.

"All that should make it easy," she said. "Besides I am
here now, to teach you."

Then she stretched out a hand to me. Whereat I cried,
as I'd not done before—nor have I done for months and
years—and when at last I looked at her I saw her own eyes
glistened.

# ❧XIII❧

Monday, June 13, 1831

As soon as the clothes were set to boiling she brought
down her pattern book—filled with sketches and hints
from friends, and various notations. I considered each one
with care and from the whole number selected three, none
of which had difficult curves, or seemed in any other way
likely to be too demanding of my present skills. From

these I chose, for two principal reasons, the one called Mariner's Compass.

1) It requires a background of white. For that I can use our old linen sheeting, already mended as far as can be, with outside edges long sewn to the centre, and some still further patched. Now that her boxes of house goods are come I need not scruple excessively over such use of ours.

2) Mariner's Compass is little known here tho' popular near Boston, and North as far as Maine. 'Tis said to be made by sailors' wives that their dear ones would be preserved, and brought safely home.

Tuesday, June 14, 1831

Saying, "Well begun were half done," she shewed me, on my return from school, where she had laid out snips and scraps collected from how many shirts and dresses and salvaged from other worn clothing. "You'll need to cut them very exact," was all I had of instruction before commencing my task.

O! if the Jew but knew the use to which I put his scissors. This cutting is a tedious matter—one must bend to it very close; also she watches over me to see that I take sufficient care in laying out the pieces that the least of the cloth be wasted.

Wednesday, June 15, 1831

A story from Uncle Jack: A farmer wagered he knew to the pound how much his grey mare could draw. A by-standing stranger selected a log. The farmer nodded, a dollar was wagered, and the mare hitched up. This time it seemed the farmer would lose, for the mare could not budge the log. Before he'd forfeit his dollar tho', the Yankee re-checked the scene. And there he discovered a pair of wet mittens lying on the log. No sooner did he lift them off than the mare moved smartly along, the farmer winning his wager.

"But is it a *true* story?" Daniel asked. "Do you think it *might* have happened? I mean, sir, would a *really* good farmer know his horse so exactly and what a mare can do?"

Thursday, June 16, 1831

Joshua surprised us, this afternoon, by meeting us at school. He had it in mind to walk down to the Shipmans' and if he was going to go that far would do it with company. His mission afforded a second surprise: Teacher Holt had said he'd find Joshua some books! And Joshua, once the most indifferent of scholars, had troubled to come this long dusty way just to claim the favour. J. now confesses he aspires to study at Mr. Dudley Leavitt's school down to Meredith.

## Saturday, June 18, 1831

Every day I must cut, trim, and sort pieces for my quilt. I thought to have had all ready by now but seem to have scarcely started. You would not think it would take so long just to prepare the work! When I remarked on my lack of progress, she quickly took the occasion to point her moral out. "Perhaps had you known what you're learning now you would not have so quickly agreed to what you did last Winter."

## Monday, June 20, 1831

I dare say it went well with Asa, since giving his verse to Sophy. Every day, this Summer term, she walks homeward with Cassie and me; and none of us mention what all of us know: the road we take is the longest way 'round to Sophy's own front door!

Lately, I notice, nearly every day, Asa, by what coincidence, finds himself at fence-side just after school lets out!

Wednesday, June 22, 1831

Nothing as we have done it before seems to satisfy her now.

"Loosen the bedsheets first from the corners; that way the strain will be less great and the wear prolonged. Catherine! Matty! Don't pull at them so! Now mind what I've told you, girls!"

She is that particular how each thing is done. Do mind this and do mind that! "Work worth doing is worth doing well," I hear at every hand.

Yet just as it seems I bring only vexation, she'll take my side 'gainst Daniel's complaint, or even caution my father, "But Charles, she's but a child!"

Yesterday I came upon her as she repacked a trunk in which she'd brought clothes out from Boston.

"Do you like these, Catherine?" she asked, holding up a set of cuffs and a matching collar.

When I allowed by word and gesture that I thought them beautiful, she said quietly they should be mine, and gave them over to me.

Thursday, June 23, 1831

We had a great storm last night! It split two trees near the West field's fence; this morning water flowed over the road like a new sprung river! Indeed, at the steps at the corner of the barn, we had an infant waterfall which lasted half the day!

I think there are few displays more grand than a Summer's thunder storm. Matty feels quite the opposite and passed the whole of last night's storm with a shawl pressed to her eyes.

Friday, June 24, 1831

With the addition of those cut today, I now have sufficient pieces to begin the figures. The background will take longer as 'tis larger in extent.

Monday, June 27, 1831

Weekday, Saturday, and Sabbath-day fly! We have very much to do, to which is added my quilting. At this I stitch and stitch away. I must give to her to approve each block as it's completed.

Lately the weather is very fine, and the evenings long. The stricture to be home by dark—which so shortens our Winter visits—hardly touches us now. Night after night our yard, or the Shipmans', rings with laughter as we engage in Blind Man's Bluff or Snap the Whip or similar diversions. Daniel and Asa have become fast friends —some times a blessing and some times not as they *will chase* after me and Cassie with some horrid toad they've caught, or garden snake they've captured.

# Hurrah for JULY THE FOURTH!

We passed the whole of this day in town, having departed just as soon as morning chores released us. The sun was not yet fully arisen—when, with packed meal beside us in the wagon, and well cooled keg of cyder beside—we five left the yard.

Even as we rumbled towards town we heard the bells begin to ring, and the firing of cannon. The streets around the green were throng'd and noisy with a million cries and small boys going every where, lustily drumming on pails. From time to time a fire cracker would explode near by. We saw two teams that nearly panicked, the horses rearing tho' confined by harness, and whinnying in terror. Babe and Nelly seemed deaf-eared throughout, and were calm all day. Some times I feel I must love these beasts for their unfailing patience, their enormous size.

Wagons and chaises surrounded the green whereon at 9 o'clock promptly the militia paraded. Presently all the marchers stopped, and stood most steadily in their places, while fife and fiddle & drummers performed, the last of their tunes being Yankee Doodle, which was the most applauded. Next was read, in ringing tones, the Declaration of Independence; this being followed by a prayer given by the militia captain. A soldier's prayer is even more forceful than one by a minister. (Perhaps 'tis the *unexpectedness* of some-time strength so sweetly gentled? I am reminded of that day when Father insisted that he alone would attend the cooking.)

Dan'l and Asa soon slipped off, and Father went with Uncle Jack to refresh himself at the tavern. However, we women wanted not for diversion, & hardly knew they were gone! The scene before us was constantly changing and, at 11 o'clock in the morning, the oration was given. A Judge J Wax came down from Plymouth especially for the event. At the end he espied two fellows with thin white hair & pipe stem legs, wearing what seemed the well-worn remains of that well-loved uniform—the buff coloured trousers & deep blue coats of General Washington's soldiers. The speaker's eager *imagination* placed them both at Valley Forge, and lauded them as *patriots* by whose *example* we might be inspired, and called on them to reply.

At this they nudged and poked each other, grinned in embarrassed toothlessness, and only later did we all learn: these were Hessians who'd served with Burgoyne and shared in his defeat!

By mid-day, it having grown quite warm, we sat beside the wagon, grateful for the wedge of shade that its height afforded. There did we eat the meal we'd brought—the outdoor air enhancing its flavour—and presently Father re-appeared to keep us company. He'd heard reports of burns, one maiming, through misfired explosions.

The afternoon hours drifted by; some who'd heard of Father's remarriage took the occasion to come around and examine his new wife. I think she came off well in this; she seemed not discomforted and replied most pleasantly as she was spoken to.

There was one final delight in the day! As we made our way towards home—weary, warm, and satisfied—I looked back over the valley. At this very moment there arose from the green a final display of fireworks against the evening sky! Even Dan'l applauded this and for once did not complain or make a fall-shy comparison with how 'tis done in Boston.

## Thursday, July 7, 1831

Very hot again today & with no prospect of rain. The raspberries are poor this year. We even consider whether 'tis worthwhile to turn them in to jam.

Because it has lately been so dry Father is in daily fear that we may suffer a fire! We've stored some buckets of water in the house and are especially careful over our cooking now.

Walking home from school today we saw how deeply our bare feet imprinted the soft and velvet dust.

The Shipman family just now left, they having passed here a pleasant visit after the supper hour.

## Friday, July 8, 1831

Matty was stung by a bee today which caused her face to swell. I noticed that she came not to me, but rather took her complaint to *her*—who quickly put her handwork down and taking Matty by the hand, led her to the Summer kitchen. There she mixed salt and water together until they formed a crusty paste which she applied to the sting.

It proved a useful remedy with which we were not acquainted.

I watched the whole of this from my stool, where I sat with churn between my knees, willing the butter to come. Later she sat with M. a while, and sang small funny songs to her. Our mother would have done the same, and did so, once, for me.

Monday, July 11, 1831

We hear they are having difficulty to raise the money to complete the Bunker Hill monument! Solicitations have been made, but fall short of the mark. Six years ago, when she took Daniel to witness the marker's dedication, General Lafayette from France and our own Senator Dan'l Webster both were there. Daniel had said they were the same because they shared the name. "And now," she exclaimed, as a story-teller will who has a particular point to make, "I proudly add that Senator Webster *also* was the son of a farmer in the state of New-Hampshire!" "Hurrah!" yelled Matty and I at this. But Daniel looked none too pleased.

Mr. Webster had given a rousing speech, as he was expected to do, being well known for declaiming. In it he said that the monument—both because of its *height* and *location*—would now greet the voyager who entered Boston harbour. Conversely, and equally fitting, he thought, it would provide the traveller, departing, with his last sight of home.

Tuesday, July 12, 1831

Daniel has found a most perfect new name by which I and Matty, too, may address his mother.

"Mammann," said he, combining her name with the common Mamma.

However, she heard it otherwise.

"Daniel," she cried, "what an elegant thought! We can say it is after the French, and thus the height of fashion."

Be that as it may, it pleased me well; also it seemed her light remark served to conceal true feeling. Later I told her, "Good night, Mammann."

It was, and both of us knew it to be, the first I'd addressed her directly.

Wednesday

Daniel is teaching me how to do sums; wherefore I plan to surprize him, next Winter, by knitting him a muffler, fringed, and dyed to the butternut's colour.

Thursday, July 14, 1831

A boy has died in Meredith, of burns received the Fourth of July, while setting off explosions. A terrible price, as Mammann says, to pay for celebration.

Father believes it will always happen—so long as the Fourth is celebrated, and *that* so long as this nation of ours holds dear the freedom on which it rests; and which we *love,* he concluded.

"You know I love it no less than you," she retorted hotly. "Still must I believe there exist other means to show our joy than those which cost us human life year after year after year."

"And do you remember Zebulon Preston?" Mr. Shipman asked. "How he got his ear blown off, and stood there with the blood running down, not knowing what had happened?"

Mammann shushed him on the spot, but I was fascinated! Mr. Preston, the flour miller, was well known to me. Often enough, while he talked with Father, I had stared at the side of his head with its furrowed scar. So that was how it came about! I had not known before.

Mrs. Preston, the miller's wife, is very pimpled and stout. But who would accept so maimed a man except she had no choice? They have many children, the eldest Matty's age.

~~Thursday~~ Friday, July 15, 1831

Beans. We eat them as they come in, at morning and evening meals. Then we shell them to spread and dry, and save against next Winter.

It seems each year it is the same. I am certain I would rejoice *never* to see more beans. Mammann says that is very short-sighted; while Father reminds us with serious voice, "For harvest and good bounty one ought give naught but thanks. Were I your teacher, Catherine," he says, "I'd have you write that out."

## Saturday, July 16

Scarcely time, these Summer nights, for keeping of a journal! I would record, if hastily, that our teacher, gentle and kind, does better with the younger pupils than we older scholars.

Cassie and I, still best of friends, have rather less to say to each other than we were wont to do. Often, now, I confide in Mammann; and Cassie and Daniel—as who would have guessed!—are plainly drawn to each other. When once I mentioned this to Cassie her quickening colour clearly confirmed what her words denied. Asa teazes her very much, which I think not kind.

## Sabbath

"They are wrong," observes Mammann, "about the swallows and Spring. It is *exactly* one of them that creates a season! Take a whole flock, overwhelming a meadow, and that is merely a lot of birds—and good grain plundered besides!"

# ❧XIV❧

Monday, July 25, 1831

Teacher Holt and Aunt Lucy Mason are going to be married! Cassie says she is older than he, but not enough to matter. They have not set the marriage date, or if the wedding will take place here or Salem, Massachusetts, which is Aunt Lucy's home.

Cassie & I are beside ourselves with hoping that our own New-Hampshire will prove the favoured location. As was decided concerning Aunt Lucy, Matty & I will call him Uncle Edward, as will the Shipman children.

We are the first, after the Shipmans, to have the happy news.

Mammann says that joyful times should as truly confirm our faith as times of sorrow test it. For good times and ill each have their place; and he who doubts or questions either will only reveal how poor is his trust, how flawed his obedience.

Thursday, July 28, 1831

As Cassie, Sophy, and I together made our way from school today, I and Cassie talked about Aunt Lucy, how happy she now seems.

"I'm tired of her and her happiness," cried Sophy on a sudden.

"How will it be, do you think for me, when I've gone to the mills. . . ? Promise you'll both remember me? And O! I shall write you letters and letters! And you must do the same!"

"Why, Sophy," Cassie answered her, "you'll be the one more likely to forget amidst new ways and company; while here 'twill always be the same, and we two merely going on in the same old ways—"

"Promise," said Sophy, "will you promise me that?"

"I promise," said Cassie seriously, surprized by this sudden emotion on our friend Sophy's part.

Then loud shouts overtook us all as Dan'l and Asa on the gallop appeared; and if they'd observed that tender moment they confessed it not. Soon, with whoops and cheerful yells, we climbed the fence and crossed the fields—the way, tho' rather rougher, being a short-cut home.


Monday, August 1, 1831

At last, last night, heavy rain! Father believes it has come too late to save the food corn, already parched, but may be preserving to some. Mammann's roses, for which she feared, stand up brightly now.

## Tuesday, August 2

When we descended the school house path who was there but Joshua! He'd been sent to salt the calves, then contrived a longer way 'round, that he'd be at the school house at the dismissal bell! He walked with me, Cassie, and Sophy talking idly of this & that, then suggested we turn through the woods, which they wished not to do. Then Josh and I parted from them, tho' not without calling back and forth with small tho' urgent messages about the coming day. Soon we felt the woodsy shadows, whereat we continued more quietly, grateful to be cool.

Were further rewarded to discover a very handsome oriole, who calmly let us approach him. We stood quite close for the longest time, observing every shaded feather; I longing the while for pen and ink that I might have drawn him from life.

Now does memory show him to me—such a handsome creature, with proud tilt to his head!

## Wednesday, August 3, 1831

The fire, our friend in Winter months, is a tyrant now! I dread to waken the coals each day; and should Dan'l murmur of sun on fields I quickly offer him turn about —to lift the kettle to the blaze, or tend full pots at the fire's edge while steaming vapours rise.

Mammann's complexion suffers altho' she does not

complain. She whose skin was white and fair has lost that elegance. Her cheeks have become as ruddy as mine, despite the bonnet she wears out of doors; and all but forgetting the demands of style, she pins up her hair like a farmer's wife and bares her arms to the elbow.

Thursday, August 4, 1831

Teacher Orpha sometimes permits the conduct of school out of doors. On these days we convene near the tree, the littlest ones gathering close to her, and some times, even, one of the babes will lay his head in her lap. "Poor little thing," she'll say with a smile. Or maybe, "Pretty dreamer!"

Then does the droning of our voices rival that of the somnolent bees while off to one side, the more wakeful infants intone their little verses, and their abc's.

For our part we're set three-syllable words, and do not tell Teacher Orpha we have mastered them before.

Bru-tish-ness.
Fruit-ful-ness.
Love-let-ter.
Jew-el-ler.

I thought about the Jew today, the scissors that he sold me, and will he come again?

*Seven* blocks of my quilt are done; so many more remain!

Friday, August 5

Dan'l and Asa, having made a pact, assisted each other in their chores, then prepared for fishing. Father watched them from afar, then came closer to where they worked to offer much and varied advice to which they listened politely.

She called after, "Do take care!" To which Dan'l made no answer. No doubt he knows how to traffick in Boston; but, concerning Nature's ways, shows himself imprudent.

Saturday, August 6, 1831—a day uncommonly hot!

The cats lie stretched on the horse-barn sill, that ancient, flat, and solid stone being shaded through the morning. Poor kitties, they are too hot to stir! I saw a mouse quick cross the floor. And Tabby, tho' she must have known, did not attempt pursuit.

We all move slowly in the heat, having still our chores to do, but secretly wishing like the tabby-cats we might lie out in repose.

Sunday, August 7, 1831

Another of Father's stories.
When he himself was but a boy, a woman who was exceedingly poor lived past Meredith Center. Her children

went barefoot most of the Winter, and often were wan and tattered.

One day the woman came to a house to ask a bit of butter. When the farm wife said that she had none, the other flew in to a rage. Shrieking coarsely, "You better had!" she ran across the yard.

Then the good wife sat down to churn, but the butter would not come. Recalling then the other's curse, the good wife brought her fire well up and having removed the pot from the crane, held the hook to the fire. When that device came to glow like the coals, she plunged it in to the churn so that steamy clouds rose up. When she resumed her churning, the butter was quickly made.

Just at sundown two days later a child came to her door. "Our mother is taken ill," cried she. "O, I do pray you to come."

Quickly the good wife put on her shawl, and went in to the night. Soon she entered the neighbour's wretched house, and tho' she dearly wished to withdraw she approached the other's bed. At once she knew it was too late and that no help could be given. The poor woman's breath soon left her body, she attended only by her piteous babes and the neighbour woman.

Our father paused as he came to this, then hushed his tone to continue.

They said in town, and for miles around, that when the body was made ready for the grave, a recent burn was discovered. Its shape was that of an old-fashioned hook, exactly the kind the good wife had used to purify the milk.

I cannot rest for thinking on it; those poor orphaned children; how came the burn to be there?

Tuesday, August 9, 1831

The weather still very extreme. Although I try to be patient, still will I complain. Mammann, should she hear me, is quick to observe I ought to be glad for our large Summer kitchen, which spares the house the worst of the heat. Or, as she said the other day, "Think you on the *city* dwellers, where every street knows a hundred fires, and there's no stream in endless fall to the trough behind the barn."

What she calls "the country life" is amazement to her still.

"Catherine," she'll say, putting hands to her hips in a favourite posture, "now just come look at this!" Or, should we be berrying, down in the patch, "Catherine, do you see that leaf, the one that's too soon painted over with the colours of autumn?" Or: "Mark that upstart flower there! I've not seen its like before!" Then she will ask how it is called; and should I not be equipt with its name she will tell me to look at it well that I may be able, once we are home, to sketch it out for Father.

Wednesday, August 10, 1831

The dark-striped tabby had four kittens today and each of them a darling! We knew her time was nearly here, but had not thought so soon.

Cassie likes the pure white one best. I prefer the little black, whose two front paws are tipped.

They are too tiny to take in our hands, and sleep so curled and sweet.

Thursday, August 11, 1831

Cassie, Mammann, Mrs. Shipman, and I were occupied nearly all of this day with picking whortleberries. The women gossiped like girls! We found a great many excellent berries and so will have both pie and pudding, the latter enriched with Summer milk, nearly as thick as cream.

Our arms, before the day was done, were criss-cross'd with welts and scratches. The berries grow so close to the briars one can not have one without the other—a lesson, I'm sure, for us to regard—but no one, not even Cassie's mother, this day pointed it out!

I know not which I enjoyed the most—the berries themselves, so plump and sweet, or, after we picked and sampled our fill, to wash ourselves in Little Squam Pond before returning home. I found the water refreshingly clear and happily not too cold. Cassie, however, became quite chilled. That is often the case with her. I noted, when we said good-bye, her hands were *still cold* to the touch.

Tomorrow we shall meet together to assort the berries we've got, and pick out the rough stems.

Friday, August 12, 1831

Perhaps having gotten too much chilled, Cassie is struck with fever. She came not to school today; and afterwards Willie came around to say they'd not be coming by as we had expected.

Daniel is in a great sulk. He wanted to go with Asa to town. But Mammann said where a town was concerned any two boys were slower than one. And would not grant permission.

Saturday, August 13, 1831

Mammann returned sorely distressed from calling on Mrs. Shipman. Cassie suddenly turned far worse and the doctor was summoned. He, to halt the progression of disease, vigourously applied his leeches. Now, as a consequence of the cure, Cassie is even more weak and pale, can scarcely sip at broth.

"But Charles," said Mammann as she put out our meal, "there must be something else to do; some other doctor to call?"

He interrupted, roughly I thought. "You forget. This is not Boston—"

"But Charles! Suppose it were one of ours—Daniel? Catherine? Little Matty? Would you say the same?"

"I told you," he said. "This is not Boston. Here we have got but just one doctor. He does his best, is all."

Monday, August 15, 1831

Again, to-day, great heat. The storm we hoped for never broke; an unfortunate circumstance.

Cassie is said to be slightly improved; I picked some flowers beside the road with hopes that I might see her. Her mother said she was resting then and would not let me in. It wasn't just the flowers though. I felt that I must speak with her, not only in my own account but with so many affectionate greetings from school mates and our teacher.

Later. Written by moonlight!

The cicadas call so loudly tonight they woke me from my sleep. How they insist that Autumn approaches; that our Summer's spent!

Tuesday

Again has Cassie taken a turn that may be for the worse. We hear that her mother resigns herself, and thus maintains composure.

"But one can see the effort, Charles! It's worse, far worse, than on Sunday! O! I can hardly bear to see—but will, of course, for I'm *resolved* to help however I can."

For a while further nothing was said. Then Mammann

spoke again. "You know that you have to fight Death, Charles . . . I have done so, and did not you? Or will you say, as you did before 'But this is not Boston?' O, Charlie, forgive me!" she said. Turned, and bolted thru the door, & quickly fled the house.

After a time Mammann returned. She had got herself composed, plaited her hair and pulled it tight, and looped it behind her ears. At once she sat down to the table and opened the writing desk. Father turned to her, surprized. Responding to his silent question, she gave no sign of the agitation she'd recently displayed. "I've decided," she explained, "to send directly to Boston to my bookseller there. I realize now that I may have need of more knowledge of remedies than I now possess."

Uncle Jack came later to visit. They sat out a while.

Wednesday, August 17, 1831

Cassie, they say, is much recovered, despite our apprehension. We are all quite gay tonight, even Mammann, I note. Perhaps, ere long and after all we will soon be berrying again, and other glad pursuits.

I saw today that the lower field, the one that borders the road to the North, is filled with laden bushes. The birds, at least, have enjoyed our absence! However, we need not be envious—the berries have lately come in thickly and are sufficient for all.

I won at spelling today.

Thursday, August 18, 1831

Last night, early, we had our storm. Afterwards Father related the story of the Old Man of the Sea. There's no one can tell a tale any better; tho' I know it well I felt actual chills at his final recital of the fatal verse:

> Man of the sea, come listen to me!
> For Alice my wife, the Plague of my life
> Has sent me to beg—a boon of thee!

Silence followed the story's end—the part when they are poor again, she having wished too high. In secret did I remember, then, that I myself had oft longed for wealth without the dint of labour. I am glad to have been set right by Father's gentle instruction, the which I perceived in the tale.

"And did that happen in Holderness, when you were a boy?"

Every one laughed aloud at poor Matty, and she rushed to the house.

Daniel arose from where he sat and quickly followed her in. I heard his voice through the open door, "Do not mind that they laughed at you; when I was small I too believed in the truth of that story. But being a boy of Boston then, I thought it happened there!"

---

Cassie is dead. It happened while she slept. I—
Saturday. August the 20th. 1831.

---

# ❧XV❧

Monday

I, Matty, and Sophy were among the twelve girls who were chosen to be in the funeral. All of us were dressed in white. We had wild flowers (the same I had picked!) in great torn armsful to carry. Josh and Zedidiah were there—Josh in a jacket too small for him—and all the Preston children.

The church bell filled the air with sound as we walked toward the cemetery. The day was so bright, and the sky so clear, it seemed to enjoin us to praise. Yet no one was there whose eyes were dry; even the men were weeping.

They say Cassie's father has composed the verse under which she will rest. It is to be a full four lines, and she should have no less:

> She lived among us for a while
> And brought joy where she went.
> We thought she was a gift of God
> But learned she was but lent.

Ever since I heard it first the tolling words repeat. I think they are so beautiful: "But learned she was but lent." I shall remember Cassie for ever—and shall strive to be good and kind, as she was, for her sake.

Thursday, August 25, 1831

We are much deprived of Mammann. She is often at Shipmans' now, to help out as she can. She is almost unnaturally calm; nor, since that day, has doubt or question been heard to cross her lips. Father, I know, and Uncle Edw. have asked Mr. Shipman can they help. But this he firmly refuses.

Resolutely, yesterday, Aunt Lucy carried out her lovely frocks—saving not a single one—to be converted to mourning clothes by means of the great dye pot. Such delicate muslins, both sprigged and plain! How well I remember when she first came, and all of us, yes Cassie too!, took such pleasure in their intricate cut or—what matters it now.

"I do not know how they do it," says Mammann. "He, Emma, all of them quiet; all of them so resigned."

One time Father tried to explain, to say that, country life being hard, country folk must learn to *accept* else they will surely be broken. Today, however, he only sighed. "I know," he said, "I know."

Friday, August 26

Merely a week ago Cassie still lived! Had I known how *few* her hours—

Perhaps 'tis better, after all, that our last parting was filled with joy, confident of the morrow.

Saturday, August 27, 1831

> We should . . . remember our departed
> friends only to imitate their virtues; and not
> to pine away with useless sorrow.
>
> Our speller, last page.

I try to be guided by these words. But I am ever mindful of Cassie; and, thinking of her, must grieve. Sophy, too, remembers. Today she said, "Remember that day when we all walked home together and I made Cassie promise to stay? How selfish I was and so unknowing, and now she's so very—so *gone* from us all."

"No!" I protested. "More with us than ever, for she lives in our thoughts and love." But that was only something to say. My heart knew Sophy right.

Later today, going after our cow, I passed the Shipmans' house. My eye flew up of its own accord to find the window, *Cassie's window*, that I once knew so well. I scarce could believe she was there no more, and never again would answer to me when I called her name from the road! There, by that ledge, we had sat so often, exchanging small, fond, secret thoughts and what foolish confessions.

Mrs. Shipman says that on that morning, when they first knew that Cassie was gone, her face was entirely peaceful. The lips, which never would speak again, were parted in a smile. Therefore, Cassie's mother says, we must also trusting be, proving thus our enduring love, and equal in our faith.

Meanwhile, Mammann awaits the stage and hopes for her book's arrival. "Suppose," she says, "it is somewhere told how to combat such illness? Then ought we not inform ourselves against another occasion?"

Mammann, Mrs. Shipman, both of them wise—yet each proposing such variant ways to confront this loss. What would my own mother have said, who did not smile with her dying breath; and whom shall I believe?

Friday, September 2, 1831

Today as I sat over my book, drawing flowers and curling ferns tho' I should have worked at my letters, David appeared at our door. I thought perhaps he had come for Dan'l. But no, this was a different errand: he'd brought such lime as we would need for preserving our eggs for the Winter. He was to tell us they'd more than enough, and would be glad to share it.

Some have whispered that Mrs. Shipman, for all that Mammann has become a friend, took unkindly M.'s poor regard for the doctor attending Cassie. I think that this is not the case, and now this kindness proves it.

The errand accomplished, D. did not leave but watched me as I picked up my pen and resumed my sketching.

"That's pretty, Cath," he said after a bit. Then taking the pen direct from my hand, he drew the dear inquisitive mouse which now peers at my daisies. I did not know he was thus inclined; only that Cassie was not "artistic," as she used to say of me.


Sunday, September 4, 1831

This morning's sermon reminded us that *great though* our grief and suffering be, others have suffered more. It is just five years since the Wiley Slide, which was made the case in point. Father, after we supped last night, recalled the tragedy.

The year was 1826, and on the mountains hereabouts there had been disturbances and troubling slides of rocks. Most concerned were those like the Wileys whose farms were perched on Crawford Notch where the mountain side climbs steeply.

On this particular afternoon the ominous rumble of distant boulders warned of avalanche. No one knows for certain what happened, or at what moment the Wileys decided to flee the imperiled house. Alas for the frailty of those persons; they perished one and all.

Their would-be rescuers found them there—caught as they were by rock and stone which coursed across once fertile fields destroying all they met. They say that some of them clutched in their hands such small possessions as they'd hoped to save: a book, a portrait, a doll.

As for the house they had lately left, it was perfectly *saved!* At that moment the avalanche had parted, roaring down on either side, neither breaking the window glass nor unhinging the gate.

Although the rescuers lost all hope, still they entered in to the house and its ghastly silence. As if that silence itself would speak, the Bible lay open on the table presenting a text which Father now found and read aloud to us:

> The Lord also thundered in the heavens,
> and the highest gave his voice; . . . then
> the channels of the waters were seen, and
> the foundations of the world were discov-
> ered at Thy rebuke, O Lord, at the blast of
> the breath of Thy nostrils.

Daniel, at the sound of this, broke into sobs, strange, racking boy's sobs, and stumbled from the room. I then remembered what I've cruelly forgot, being turned in upon myself: he loved Cassie too.

Monday, September 5, 1831

While the washday kettles boiled this morning I took time to assist Mammann in tying up our herbs. Earlier we had picked them over, assorting them as to kind. Tansy we had in goodly amount, and pepper—and spearmint both. (She especially favours a peppermint tea, strongly brewed to settle the stomach, or when we are looking peaked.) Also we had our sassafrass roots, and comfrey from the garden.

Later, Asa and David came by to visit with Dan'l a

while. They three have grown rather closer together, and some times will let me join with them, now that Cassie's gone.

# ❧XVI❧

Tuesday, September 6, 1831

I have fallen far behind on my stints of piecing. Mammann said I might not do else but put more time to sewing.

"Has it a name, this quilt of yours?" David asked today.

"Mariner's Compass," I quickly replied, demonstrating the pattern. "Mammann had planned to make such a quilt before she came to us." Then I told them, as she'd told me, the story of its meaning.

"But how would it avail," Asa asked, "with the quilt in Boston and the sailor on the sea?"

"O, come now, Asa, 'tis not meant so!" But I laughed, despite myself, and so did the others who heard.

All at once it came to me: this was the first we had laughed aloud ~~since it happened~~ since Cassie died.

Wednesday, September 7, 1831

Today Matty played with her dolls! She had not done so in ever so long; there were some I had quite forgotten, to whom I apologized. They had got in such disarray! We dressed them out as best we could; even Mammann sat down with us, and improvised a tiny bonnet from a dimity scrap.

I remember when I used to play, every day & for hours and hours. But that was long ago, of course, when I was very small.

Thursday, September 8, 1831

The kittens are finding their way about, having grown quite large. I came on the white one in the field, already hunting alone! It has wonderful jade green eyes, and is quick and cunning.

Monday, September 12, 1831

Father very weary tonight; an ancient injury causes him pain, but he will do nothing about it. We know that he was determined—and is—to complete the haying before he slacks his pace.

"There are more of us now, to house and feed. And

goodness knows," this to Mammann, "you've risked enough in coming here—" He did not finish the thought.

I wonder does he think some times, of the one with whom long ago he began this house? Certainly I, 'midst the mourning of Cassie, was *reminded* of those other dark days—when the bed room mirror was turned to the wall and I woke one morning to the smell of cut wood and two new-made coffins. Hers was so large, and the baby's so small, and both of them in the house.

Tuesday, September 13, 1831

Tonight we learned there has been a revolt of Negro slaves in the South. The Boston papers tell of nothing else. Many people were cruelly murdered, including women & children. Most of the slaves have been taken and shot. The leaders, Nat Turner the chiefest of these, are secured in jail.

It happened on August 21, the day after Cassie died. Strange, that one speaks of these deaths and slayings and is not disposed to tears. Yet each of those who perished there was to some other one dear.

Mammann says we mourn all deaths with each particular grief. Are we then with those strangers joined whose lives, names, faces are veiled from us yet whose griefs we share? Is this what Mr. Garrison meant when he penned the motto: "our countrymen all mankind?" I think once more of the Wiley Slide. How can what we call *Providence* so oft, so cruelly, deprive?

Wednesday, September 14, 1831

More on the Insurrection.

Uncle Jack has today obtained the newest *Liberator*. Of the recent slave rebellion Mr. Garrison there records that "what was prophesied in January has now become a bloody reality." The Editor states, as could he not, that the killings were a dreadful event. Nevertheless, concerning the raiders, he believes "[they] deserve no more censure than the Greeks in destroying the Turks, or the Poles in exterminating the Russians, or our fathers in slaughtering the British."

To read in this way of the War of Independence was shocking to us all. Mammann said that she'd no more have that paper in this house.

There was a hurricane in Port-au-Prince. Seven *hundred* died.

Thursday

Talk occasioned by the slaves' revolt continues unabated. *Many* now favour the establishment of a *new Negro separate* nation, it to be called Liberia and in Africa. Opposition, as might be expected, comes largely from the Southern owners of the large plantations. They are dependent upon the Blacks for free & diligent labour. The reasons put forth are various, some of them humane. They say, for example, the slaves are ill-prepared, being by now dependent on their masters for so much of their care.

Also, some slaves have no *wish* to go; and shall they be deported even against their will? 'Twould be as cruel as the situation which first brought them here!

Father, for all this, says he approves of the resettlement movement. Uncle Jack, to our surprize, quite fervently disagrees. It seems to him that Southerners, having the greater *connection* with Negroes, ought to know better what's good for *them* than we Yankee farmers.

In my mind I am now quite certain. The fugitive was a run-away slave, and could have been no other.


Friday, September 16, 1831

Haying, mowing, gathering in! Daniel works hard, along side of Father, and declares he sincerely looks forward to the resumption of school.

Father accepts this good humouredly. "I told you we'd make a farm boy of him and must be that we've done so!"

"How is that?" Mammann inquires, looking up from her work.

"I never knew a farm boy yet who'd not trade hay-fork for quill and ink at this particular season!"


Saturday, September 17, 1831

Last night we had scarce retired when a display of Northern lights called us from our beds. It was a most impressive display, being very especially clear tho' rather less in colour than others we have seen. At their height the lights spanned the sky, flinging great arcs of shimmering light clear to the Western horizon! Then their nature utterly changed and, like a gossamer veil or curtain, they gently rippled and undulated across their entire range.

We must have watched an hour or more before they began to dim. Whereat we knew our weariness and once again bid all good night, and soon as I blow my candle out, I know sweet sleep will discover me, and I welcome him.


Monday, September 19, 1831

We hear that Aunt Lucy's marriage date, delayed because of Cassie's death, is now again put forward. Teacher Holt has accepted a position ("I should think he would," our father approves) at the boys' academy down to Exeter. Aunt Lucy and he are in haste to remove, that they may *establish* themselves before the Autumn term.

'Tis Aunt Lucy's wish to be married here, where joy and love and sorrow have come, each of them in turn. The Shipmans have consented, tho' were opposed at first.


Tuesday, September 20, 1831

Mammann disciplined Matty today, M. having protested a favour that Mammann had asked. It was

Mammann's contention that, "You must learn to like the doing of that which we like you to do. Glad submission of the will," she explained, "is the obedience that proves control. I do not mean you merely to comply. Reflect, accept, obey!"

How I used to struggle with Matty, and on this account. Discipline of will, not relinquishment, is the lesson's desired end. How hard this is for each to learn, and how necessary.

Tomorrow Sophy will leave for Lowell. Mammann has said we may walk to the bridge, there to observe her departure, and to wish her good speed.

# ❧XVII❧

Wednesday, September 21, 1831

With many a tear did we wave Sophy off, she who mounted the stage steps bravely, two days past the end of the term and scarce more since her birthday. Many a keepsake was presented to her. But I observed she had pinned to her bodice a tiny ring of braided hair; Asa's by the colour.

I had not known how dear you had become. Dear Sophy! I wish you well.


## Thursday, September 22

Aunt Lucy's wedding will take place on Sunday; sooner than we thought! Mammann once asked will I wear the bonnet which she sent from Boston and which is still untried. I would like to do it, to please her; but cannot, will not, won't.


## The Sabbath and a Wedding!

Aunt Lucy's marriage was celebrated on this very day! Scarcely any were gathered there who'd not been present short weeks ago when Cassie was laid to rest. All the Shipmans were dressed in black—save Aunt Lucy in bridal white, to which some gave poor comment.

I wore my Sunday-best printed muslin, and a brooch, once my own mother's, to fasten up the throat. Father wore his wedding jacket—very handsome, I must say—as was Mammann, her hand on his arm, in her dark green silk.

The ceremony was very brief—truly I think we have never been so short a time in church!

Some item of business having been forgotten, scarce had the newly-wed pair gone off, but that they returned!

Cheers, jeers, and laughter greeted them, and Mr. Perkins called out, "Had enough already?"

"No, sir!" Uncle E. shot back. "But after so fine a wedding trip I thought to try another!"

Aunt Lucy blushed most prettily; and this time when they started off we knew they were gone to stay.


Thursday, September 29, 1831

Today, through the post, came a packet to me labelled in the same crude hand that once had spoken a run-away's need, to which our quilt had answered.

I had not thought to see again those square, crude, awkward letters. Yet in an instant I sensed, I *knew*, the signer and the source. Hastily I undid the seals. The opened package disclosed to me two matched pieces of crocheted lace; and once again that writing.

SISTERS BLESS YOU.
FREE NOW. CURTIS.

IN CANADA

Thus all doubts were settled.

The man we had helped had indeed been a slave; and having been neither fugitive nor phantom, was now in Canada. Free!

But: Sisters? I puzzled. And *two* bits of lace? Then how bitterly did I weep. One was meant for Cassie.

Wednesday, October 12, 1831!

The start of Winter school. I walked with Matty, Dan'l, and Asa—but far more mindful of those now gone than my present companions.

Mammann gave me a shawl of her own. "That colour becomes you well," she said, and placed it across my shoulders, knotting it in front. For just a moment her eyes caught mine, yet neither of us could speak aloud the thoughts so deeply felt.

This year some scholars are smaller than Matty! She, so proudly promoted, sits on the second bench!

Concerning the teacher, I like him not. His face is triangular, small, and pinched. He sniffs and coughs for emphasis, and to conclude each statement. 'Tis painful to think of dear Teacher Orpha, also of Uncle Edward Holt, who occupied this place.

The older boys are wary already, and who could fail to observe the switches leaning in the corner? Seven new ones, all freshly cut. And he made plain (sniff) that he meant (hm-hm) to use them (hm-hm) to keep order.

Joshua was there whom I have not seen since Cassie's funeral.

Thursday, October 13, 1831

Sophie's father intends them all to remove to Ohio in the early Spring! He is told there's good land to be had by those who'd try homesteading. Also he is weary with the ragged, pick-stone farm he has; and the cruel climate. As for

Sophy's wages, says he, let them be spent where there is *hope;* here he finds no encouragement and small return for his labours. Sophy's mother, and her brother, will not go with him directly. Rather they'll stay till a homestead is reached, and a cabin built.

I try to suppose what I would do were we to announce such a plan. But there is little danger thereof; Father being so very attached, Mammann so lately arrived.

Friday, October 14, 1831

The stencillers were here today, having completed their Northerly circuit—all the way to North Parsonfield, in the State of Maine! Now, with the geese, they make their way to a warmer clime.

They had stopped at the Shipmans' first, where, as they said, they were greatly saddened to learn of the recent loss. "She was a lovely bit of a thing; sad, how they go," the older one said, "and so often taken in Summer."

Tho' Father said plain he'd no money for murals they shewed no intention to leave. After a time the bearded one spoke. "Got you a wife since we've been here." "And a son besides," adds Father.

"A *full-grown* son," the elder revised, and after a moment's contemplation winked at Father to elaborate the thought that lay at the heart of the jest. "A few months married and a full-grown son!" he pronounced with evident glee, evoking general laughter.

One way and another it came about that the painter himself would attempt a likeness of the new Mistress Hall. Using the new *camera obscura* would so greatly speed the process, a dollar only would he charge; and Father at no extra cost might, himself, employ the device for portraits of "the children."

So it was bargained and so it was done. Laughing, we each of us took our turn at sitting before this strange device—a large black box whose inner workings deploy the light by a careful arrangement of a series of mirrors. Then, as he showed us, a special lens, directs the image upon a paper—which has been placed, or so arranged, that the image may be traced, and then coloured in.

This last, it appears, is greatly dependent on the skills of the portrait maker. Tho' *Mammann's* likeness is good indeed, the ones of us that Father made are difficult to admire. Mine, I think, is the worst of all! My brow appears unnaturally broad, my chin is but a nubbin!

Sunday, October 16, 1831

Fallen leaves are every where, and every where, too, the spicy scent of newly gathered apples. Soon they shall be milled into cyder, for the Winter's pleasure.

Our Uncle Jack, whom we saw after church, speaks with approval of Mr. Perkins, and says he might do the same. We can not tell if he jests or not; but Uncle Jack says he's just found out he has a hankering for Ohio or some place to the West.

Once, a while ago, he said, "You've got Daniel now for help." Another time, as I recall: "At times I think the best I grow is granite stones for fences."

Since Mammann's arrival here, he visits us less often. It seems he's often ill at ease, and like as not her influence with Father must diminish his own.

I have determined to read from the Bible; some lines every day.

Monday, October 17, 1831

They say the Jew was in Meredith lately; however, we did not see him. Perhaps he's in haste for the homeward journey, it being now late in the season and the nights already cold.

From our speller: Zeno, hearing a young man very loquacious, told him that men have two ears but one tongue; therefore ought they hear twice as much as they intend to speak.

Thursday, October 20, 1831

Father down to the cyder mill today, also to Holderness. Mammann's book of remedies is come; also the bookseller calls to her notice a volume intended as the "poor man's friend" and prepared *especially for those* who've settled in the Western regions and *other lands and territories where doctors are not to be had. Gunn's Domestic Medicine* was only published a year ago and claims "the latest and most approved" treatments for every domestic need. Mammann says she'll consider the purchase, although 'tis priced quite dear.

Father has learned that it is being said we've the best kept school in the district. Therefore are the committee pleased; who would be less so, I stoutly maintain, were theirs the scholar's place.

Each day, it seems, new rules are announced; and punishments for their flouting. David, Josh, Dan'l, & Asa—nearly all of the older boys—seem determined to try him. They smirk and murmur with insolence, sprawling their legs when his back is turned & noisily rocking the benches if they've got uneven legs. Thus do they fairly *invite* a whipping, which he threatens but does not perform. I swear I know not where all will end, but do not like the flavour.

Sunday, October 23, 1831

This year's harvest being done this day, Father gave Daniel the Barlow knife that was his as a boy. Much did he say concerning its use, and that there is nothing like a Barlow knife to turn an idle hour to a worthwhile cause. But I, remembering the infant Nathaniel, & my father's words to him, knew there was more unspoken: now does the present re-pay the past and flow on towards the future.

Some times, long before Dan'l came, I used to wonder if I might have Father's knife . . .

Monday, October 24, 1831

O, I do think, as has been said, that if getting in the corn and potatoes are the prose of a farm child's life, then nutting's the poetry!

Chestnuts and beechnuts are plentiful now, and some hickories. Also, happily in *good* supply, are those which are my especial delight, the rich, round butternuts.

The woods these days are glorious and gold, but there still hover over meadow grasses small bright butterflies. Could these sweet hours but stay & stay, cruel Winter never come nigh! No, it cannot be. Already we draw to the evening fire—first for its warmth and then for its light on these shorten'd days.

Close by the hearth I work on my quilt; Matty some times assisting me—her long wool stockings being newly completed—and Mammann says she may.

"My three girls," says Father, smiling. And Mammann colours, and quick goes on about the rug she plans to hook to her own design. She says the house needs waking to colour, and more warmth underfoot. The rug is to show a wreath of flowers, each being one that she has seen, or plucked, since coming here.

Tuesday, October 25, 1831

How shall I begin to tell it—all my forecasts answered and more—concerning the teacher's rage! Joshua was at the centre of it, for he provoked the punishment by rising from his place & desk before he was given dismissal. Add to this that he showed no shame when he was reprimanded.

"Well, then, sirrah!" &c, &c and, as Josh is taller than the teacher, he made him seem a strutting bantam, squawking out his indignation to an indifferent rooster. The hush in the room was as never before; even the littlest scholars in the room stayed their pens from paper, their chalk bits from their slates. Then, unhappily, a giggle burst forth—

Now was the teacher beside himself, and tho' this last was not Joshua's doing, Josh was called to the front of the room while, with elaborate display, the teacher chose several switches and laid them on his desk.

Meanwhile he was harangueing us: "Mark you this!" and "Mock not that!" and never was heard a sniff or cough, so fast the epithets flew!

At last a switch was taken to hand, and the teacher's sleeve rolled up. Then J. was told to remove his shirt, and present his back to the room. He was far from grinning now but seemed to me rather grimly determined to see the punishment through. Every breath was held, I believe —mine for a certainty!

"*Are you contrite?*" the teacher roared, and lifted up his arm.

Whereat, and so fast we were all amazed, David & Asa

bounded forth and seized the teacher, one to each side!, while Dan'l leap'd from the back of the room and opened wide the door. At which, in an instant, *all* the boys pelted to the front of the room, *bodily* lifted the teacher up, and *pitched* him in to the yard!

Nothing was said of this at home, yet surely the news reached Father. Dan'l, I swear, suffers more with Father's silence than all the teacher's wrath.

# ❧XVIII❧

Wednesday, October 26, 1831

With what amazement did Dan'l and I hear our father describe as a prank Monday's happening. Meanwhile, Mammann has firmly decided that neither Matty nor I, her daughters(!), shall continue to be exposed to such "common cruelty" on a teacher's part. Consequent to all of which, Matty and I are withdrawn from school, starting this very day!

So we were told on arriving home, Mammann & Father awaiting our return with news of their decision. Mammann says *she* will continue our instruction. " 'Tis not for naught I'm a teacher," she says, and has already written to Boston for the needed books. (Dear Mammann, with her faith in books and ever ready pen!) Dan'l was to have studied with us; however, pleading his loyalty to Asa, David, and other boys, he has gained reluctant consent to continue at school. Matty thinks it a holiday, for all I heard her "splain" to Asa about "our Mammann" who was once a "real teacher and not just for Summer term."

Thursday

One would think it a school house-ful instead of just two girls. Mammann announced, when breakfast was cleared, that she will set the lessons for us every morning early. Then we are to have two hours to study. After that she will hear us, and provide correction. Today's attempt—perhaps being the first—was surely comical. "At what age (Catherine, my scissors, please!) was Pocahontas when Captain John Smith fell into the Indians' hands?" And scarcely had I answered "Twelve," but that she turned to Matty with the Moral Catechism. "What is justice?" (It is giving every man his due.) "What is generosity?" (It is some act of kindness performed for another which strict justice does not demand.) "What is gratitude?" (Gratitude is a thankfulness of heart for favours received.) Today, however, the familiar words were mixed with exclamations. "Dear child, do raise up the pot!" "Matty, that sauce is going to scorch!" "Catherine, watch your stitches!"

Friday, October 28, 1831

Aunt Lucy Holt is going to have a baby in early Spring! Mrs. Shipman told Mammann this very afternoon.

Saturday, October 29, 1831

Nearly the whole of my quilt is pieced. Mammann says we must hold a quilting, and that she will speak to Father soon, whether the quilting frame will serve, or does it need repair.

Sunday, October 30, 1831

Father sat down near me today, just as the Sabbath ended. I had spread my quilt blocks out, assessing them for joining. After a bit he looked at me, clear. "Your mother would be glad of this." I knew not how to answer. Presently, thoughtful, he commenced again. This time he had more to say, and which I must try to record exact for what came afterwards.

"It was an apt choice," he began, "for are we not, all of us, wand'rers and strangers; and do we not, all of us, travel in danger or voyage uncharted seas?"

At once I saw he meant my stranger—who was safe, all

hazards survived. And Cassie, too, who had been called on a greater journey, to rest on the opposite shore.

Do I blaspheme to join them thus—the one so fair, the other so dark? one dear, and one a stranger? I do now believe we *all* are joined, where ever we are, what ever we do—and be we quick, or be we dead; fair, dark, dear, or stranger.

Monday, October 31, 1831

Today, at last, was I prepared to attend to the freeman's lace—at once a sad remembrance and happy messenger.

While my tears ran freely down I laid his gift beside her grave, wrapping with it *scented flowers* which we'd dried at Summer's close—lavender and petals of rose and spiced geranium.

I have told no one what I have done; nor need to, knowing it right.

Tuesday, November 8, 1831

Sophy, once so flibbertigibbet, sends good earnings home. All of the mill girls protested their pay, and as 'tis known no girl in New-England would take a place till the issue's resolved, the owners knuckled under rather than stop the mill.

Perhaps when I attain fifteen—younger than that I may not go—I shall join Sophy in Lowell. Unless, by then, she is in Ohio! Which may be the case.

Thursday, November 10

She is helping me to knit a cap for Aunt Lucy's baby! All the stitches must be just so, and as we are using the finest of threads this is woeful hard.

I wonder, when the baby is born, if they'll name her for Cassie, if it is a girl?

Wednesday, November 23, 1831

Because they are so lately bereaved, we did not engage the Shipmans in Thanksgiving Day. Neither, therefore, did we feast. But going to church I wore my blue bonnet—its colour a complement to my blue collar and, as was intended, to the blue of my eyes.

Monday, December 12, 1831

Father says he must be certain to purchase our Leavitt's *Almanac* for 1832! Others have spoken with favour of others. But we buy Mr. Leavitt's, he being of this county and a some-time acquaintance besides.

Monday, December 19, 1831

### Portion of a Letter Received by
### Mrs. Shipman

(It is from Aunt Lucy Holt and, because it concerns me so greatly, Mrs. Shipman has given it to me and I, for its safekeeping, thought to attach it here.)
—and would you please inquire of her parents whether Catherine might come to us after the baby is born? I believe her help will be very much needed. I am greatly alone (no friends) and we think her qualified.

The Academy admits no females as you know; the District School is poor. But Edward remembers that C. is quite clever, & would give her private instruction in the usual courses of study. This we propose to regard as exchange for the services she provides. We would assure her attendance to church, and good attention to health.

She will find this a studious house. Edw. reads so beautifully! Every evening, from eight o'clock till ten, he engages us in study! I know I can not begin to tell you the bliss of these short hours! We have already read much in French, and some philosophy.

We beg the favour of an early reply concerning Catherine's coming. You can provide our address to her parents. And do encourage them!


At the start of this journal I wrote of my wish to stay here for ever and ever; also that I wished to become better and more gladly able to do what I am asked. Today, reflecting on Aunt Lucy's letter, I know I shall find good consequence in what ever is decided by Father and Mammann. Thus it now appears to me that trust, and not submission, defines obedience.


Tuesday, December 20, 1831

I, who've not travelled past Concord and Keene, am to take up residence hours and hours away! It is the wish of Father and Mammann that I accept Aunt Lucy's post and they will inform her by letter.

I will have ample time to prepare, the baby's not due to be born until Spring. Father says I am fortunate; I need not travel till snow and ice—and mud!—will have left the road.

Friday, December 23, 1831

Mrs. Shipman confided to us she's put away for ever the clothes that Cassie wore. She worries that some might consider this wasteful, there being good wear in them yet. But Mammann spoke right out and said that what she'd done was right.


New Year's Day, 1832

How swiftly the year has turned. Winter found Spring and Spring became Summer and, as Priest Fowle reminded us:

> To every thing there is a season,
> And a time to every purpose under the
> heaven; . . .
> A time to weep, and a time to laugh;
> A time to mourn, and a time to dance—

This year, more than others, has been a lengthy gathering of days wherein we lived, we loved, were moved; learned how to accept.


Saturday, January 14, 1832

Today I stood in the Shipmans' house, my eye admiring the painted scene which Cassie herself had shown me not many months ago. There were the elms in tiny leaf, making it Spring for ever, she'd said. And so it was and so it is. For tho' the wind is bitter outside, for Cassie it is Spring for ever, nor shall she leave that season.

Later some words neither sought nor remembered presented themselves to mind:

> Now let ev'ry occasion fill,
> Command thy heart to joy.

Can it be some hymn once sung, imprinted on my infant sense although not comprehended? Where come such words? From my own self? Glad, although not unafraid, I am determined to obey, believing that only the *form* of instruction is *mysterious*.

Friday, February 3, 1832

Heavy snow. Knitted all afternoon.

Sabbath

Snow again. Could not go out.

## Tuesday, February 7, 1832

We expect the breaking out—it will be the first for Dan'l, the second time for me! 'Tis hard to think he was not here—no, nor even known to us, to share the last occasion!

## Thursday, March 8, 1832

I am to leave at daybreak and can not sleep tonight. Thus I have stolen down the stairs—their every, rough edge known to me—to sit by a single candle's light with this, my companion, my journal. I wonder if it is common to feel that never is a place so loved as when one has to leave it?

There, near the door, my two trunks wait and folded atop them is my travelling cloak; also the novel *Northwood* by Mrs. Sarah Josepha Hale. This is a gift to me, from Mammann. She ordered it from Boston. Father made much of the weight of my luggage and said that anyway he believed I would be home by Summer.

Yet now is the night still, dark, and cold. The fire has long since turned to ash with only the back log glowing. In the next room lie Father and Mammann while in the loft above me Dan'l dreams his farmboy dreams and Matty—I have no doubt of it!—allows herself excursion in to my half of the bed. The very thought recalls me!

Good night dear place, dear house, dear all—good night, and now good-bye.

Providence, R. I.
December 9, 1899

My very dear Catherine,

I am so grateful for your letter, and glad to know you enjoyed the journal I kept when a girl.

You ask about the run-away slave, he who was certainly not a phantom but a real tho' tiny part of what was happening every where then, and what was going to come. I never heard from him again, tho' some times, indeed for years and years, I used to imagine what I would do were there a knock upon the door and there he was: Curtis. He never came, of course.

Joshua Nelson stayed on as a farmer. Two of his boys went off to fight in the War between the States. One, the younger boy I think, got killed at Gettysburg. Then Josh signed up to take his place and got wounded pretty bad. It never healed the way it should, him not being young at the time. He died a couple of years ago. We exchanged Christmas cards right up to the end.

All of the others are gone now too—except for me and Little Willie Shipman. I still think of him that way although the last I heard of him someone was making a party, him turning 75!

No, I didn't forget to tell! We had no presents at

Christmas—then, nor at birthdays either. The first I saw a Christmas tree must have been in Boston and I was about 23.

Well, I am going on 83 now but not about to quit. There are too many things I know about where I want to see what happens. You, my dear, being one of them, and this new century starting.

Do what you can to make it good. And remember, as we used to say, that life is like a pudding: it takes both the salt and the sugar to make a really good one.

Lovingly, your great-grandmother,
Catherine Onesti

P.S. Thank you for telling me about the chair, that it is not worn too badly. After Mammann and Father died it went to my sister Matty. Matty never had children, though, and her husband died before her. So when she passed on, it came back to me, and I, having no use for it then, gave it to your mother. You were very clever to have figured that out.

C.H.O.

# Author's Note

A few miles north of Meredith, New Hampshire, a blacktop road cuts off to the left, and if it ever had a name no one uses it now. After gently climbing for a mile or more, it passes the site upon which stood the farm I have called the Shipmans'. Here a dirt road enters from the right and, traveling north for a few hundred yards, arrives at the house and barn, both restored, where the story takes place.

How much of it is true? I started with a handful of facts, an amateur's interest in the history of the region, and the intention to reconstruct life as it was when the house was new. To do this I worked with documents and books and newspapers of the region, visited museums and small collections, and even explored old graveyards in search of further clues. Some of the journal's episodes are freely adapted from sources consulted, among them the teacher's bodily ouster and the Count of Meredith's surprising and stylish return. But little by little the figures I imagined became more real than the rest.

One August afternoon, when I had been working on the story for some hours, I wandered into the living room—cool, dark, and familiar. There I had the distinct impression that I had somehow intruded, in time as well as in place. The house belonged, as it always would, to the people who had built it. The Catherines and Cassies, whatever their true names, had never really left. I had only filled in the story. And that is the truth.

J.W.B.
March 1979